'Nobody seems to know what's happened to him. Until two days ago his signal was coming through loud and clear, and then he . . . he just vanished!'

Zak Anderson, aged sixteen and a newly qualified space pilot, is determined to find his father – missing in unexplored space.

By a strange accident Zak and his friends find themselves in a far-off galaxy, on an unknown planet. . .

Copyright © 1983 Chris Spencer

Published by
Lion Publishing plc
Icknield Way, Tring, Herts, England
ISBN 0 85648 498 9
Lion Publishing Corporation
10885 Textile Road, Ypsilanti, Michigan 48197, USA
ISBN 0 85648 498 9
Albatross Books
PO Box 320, Sutherland, NSW 2232, Australia
ISBN 0 86760 309 7

First edition 1983

Cover illustration: Merv Jones

British Library Cataloguing in Publication Data

Spencer, Chris
    Starforce red alert.
    I. Title
    823'.914[J]   PZ7

    ISBN 0-85648-498-9

Printed and bound in Great Britain
by Collins, Glasgow

STARFORCE RED ALERT

CHRIS SPENCER

A LION PAPERBACK

To Jan

*Dedicated with thanks
to Jonathan, Carol, Lance,
George and Elizabeth*

*'He made the stars also.'
Genesis 1:16*

1

There was a sign on the wall that said 'Do Not Run', but even lead boots wouldn't have kept his feet on the ground.

'Hey, Tom!' he called out. 'Tom, I passed. I got my wings!'

The younger boy turned, a smile on his freckled face.

'You did?' And as he let out an excited whoop he clenched his fist and punched at the air.

It was the wrong thing to do in the low-gravity environment of Moon City, and he found himself taking off in the same slow-motion manner as his team-mate bounding towards him.

Four seconds later and three feet from the ground they met in a delayed-action collision and fell awkwardly to the ground, a tangle of limbs and a bundle of bruises.

When finally they came to rest, heaped up beside the automatic doors, they could not speak for laughing. Almost the very same thing had happened six weeks earlier when they had first arrived at the moon's Space Training Centre (in Zak's case to complete his studies) and on that occasion the Lunar Police had caught them. After a telling off from their group leader they had vowed never again to break the golden rule, but right now they couldn't have cared less. Zak had got his space wings! Four years with the Houston Aerospace Academy had paid off and soon he would be zipping around the universe at the controls of a space ferry.

And besides, tomorrow they would be going home!

'Whoopee!' said Tom, this time with a little more restraint. 'Good on you, Zak!' And between the last of the chuckles he prompted his pal to produce the evidence.

They untangled themselves and leaned back against the corridor wall. Still smiling, the older boy fumbled with the breast pocket of his ground-suit and eventually produced a small plastic card. He sat looking at it for a moment, wallowing in the sheer pleasure of owning it, and then he handed it to Tom.

Across the top, in angular gold lettering, was the legend STAR-FORCE COMMAND, and underneath, in computer print, was the simple but staggering announcement: Zak Anderson, Pilot, Grade III. Beneath that, not five minutes old, was the flowing signature of Charles Fairburn, Commander-in-Chief.

'Cor!' was all that Tom could say.

Zak spent a few moments soaking up this profound statement from his friend, and then he said, 'Don't worry, it'll be your turn one day.'

The younger boy handed back the card, the last trace of his smile barely hanging on.

'Yeah – but two years . . .'

'It'll soon go,' said Zak, but that didn't seem to help. Then there was an awkward pause before Zak said brightly, 'Come on, let's go and find the girls.'

As usual after the day's training they found Eve and Becky drinking milk-shakes at The Moonbeam coffee bar. But today, because it was their last, and because Eve had already found out about Zak's appointment, the table was laid with a tantalizing selection of cakes and buns.

'Oh boy! Lunar eclairs!' exclaimed Zak.

'Congratulations!' chorused the girls, and Eve stood up and threw her arms around him. She thought she would like to kiss him too, but she knew that would embarrass him, especially in front of Becky.

'You knew!' laughed Zak, wriggling out of Eve's arms as quickly as was decent.

Eve nodded, a huge, adoring smile creasing her face.

'I asked Captain Malone,' she confessed. 'He said he couldn't tell me outright whether or not you would be selected, but he said if I wanted to go ahead and arrange a slap-up tea he didn't think I'd be wasting my money.'

Zak laughed out loud. 'You mean he knew all along? Wow, I

thought I'd fluffed that last exercise – you know, when I had to dock the ship at the space station. But he must have reckoned I did all right.'

'I knew you could do it, Zak,' said Becky, beaming up at her brother, and she leaned over and pecked him on the cheek. *She* didn't care if she embarrassed him!

Tom sniggered at the expression on Zak's face, and as they settled around the table he said, 'Well, come on, then – let's get started. I'm going to have one of these Moon City Specials. Lovely!'

They watched as he sank his teeth into the crescent-shaped bun . . . and laughed as the cream squirted out and curled up over his nose.

It was a good tea, full of fun and friendship, but edged with just a tinge of regret. It was always sad when a member of your team moved on (especially when it was your brother, thought Becky). That was the only drawback to a system which dictated that the four members of each team should be of staggered ages: by the end of each year one of the team would have completed the four-year course and be posted to a position within the ranks of Starforce Command.

And now it was Zak's turn. They would miss him. They had all grown to like Zak . . . and in Eve's case it was a little more than that. Being just a year younger she had now completed three years in his team, and over that period (which now seemed far too short) she'd become very fond of him. Zak was good fun and yet he was no fool. Of course, you had to be bright to win a place at the Academy, but there was something else about Zak which Eve admired: he was resourceful and . . . well, yes – brave.

Eve would never forget that time during their previous session on the moon when they had been out in space, learning about emergency repairs to the rocket motors; the time Captain Malone had got into difficulty. They'd all been out there, floating about in their spacesuits, and any one of them could have reached him, but when the Captain's oxygen pipe got caught up in the works and was severed, it was Zak who went to his aid and seemed to know exactly what to do. It entailed breaking into his own air supply and linking it up with the officer's so that they could share Zak's tank until they were safely back inside the ship.

'Another five seconds and I would have been a chunk of space debris,' Captain Malone had joked afterwards, and he had reached out and gripped Zak's hand. 'I owe you, son. Tell me, how did you know what to do?'

'Oh, I saw some guys do it in a movie one time,' had been Zak's reply. The Captain had guessed the real answer, but in secret he understood and he wasn't going to press it.

Eve was intrigued, however, and she had pestered Zak for the truth. With much diffidence he had finally confided in her. 'Look, it was nothing. Just a little trick my dad taught me. But for Pete's sake keep it to yourself.'

She had not known what to make of that. Why should he want to keep such a thing secret? So puzzled was she that she broke the confidence and shared it with Becky. It didn't seem so bad, as Becky was Zak's sister. The younger girl had laughed.

'Oh, that's because Zak is determined to make it on his own merit. He's afraid that having a famous astronaut for a father will influence his reports – you know: that they'll think he's bound to succeed because of who he is.'

'Forgive me,' Eve had said, 'but I don't understand. Is your father well known?'

Again Becky had laughed. 'Hey, that shows just how successful Zak has been about keeping it quiet. Yes, our father is Roy Anderson.'

Eve's eyes widened.

'Roy Anderson? The first man to walk on Mars?'

'Just keep it to yourself – please. Zak's going to make it, I know he is. One day he'll have his wings, and it *will* be his own doing.'

And that's just how it had turned out.

'Do you think we'll ever get a chance to fly together again?' asked Eve, casting a wistful glance at Zak.

'Sure we will.' Zak was buoyant, but as he looked at each of his friends in turn he knew they weren't so hopeful. With good reason.

Starforce Command, which had its interplanetary headquarters in Moon City, was the western world's space security force and employed close on half a million people. On earth, where half of that number was stationed, there were bases in twelve countries. The other quarter of a million personnel were scattered across earth's solar system on colonized planets and in floating space stations. Many thousands were constantly on the move, patrolling the space lanes, escorting space ferries, guarding new space development projects, and so on. Some were engaged in missions that kept them spaceborne for months on end. So the chances of four friends out of half a million being thrown together for a tour of duty were, they knew, remote.

The fact was that once they'd split up they might not see one another again for many months. Years, even. Especially now that relations between east and west were so strained. All it needed was one act of aggression from either side and the world could find itself plunged into another space war. Once that happened there was just no telling how long it would be before they could get together again.

All of this had rushed through their minds in response to Zak's optimism, and of course Zak himself was well aware of the cloud that hung over their future. But as he sat there studying his friends' faces he was determined to lift the gloom.

'Look, I've got a great idea,' he announced breezily. 'As from tomorrow we're all on leave. Let's borrow my dad's private space-cruiser and take a vacation together. The cruiser's here on the moon. What d'you say?'

'Fantastic!' said Tom.

'Oh, yes – a holiday in space!' smiled Eve, her bright eyes sparkling at the thought of it. And she tossed back her head, laughing. 'Stars, here we come!' She turned to Becky.

'Wouldn't that be great?'

But Zak's sister was not smiling. She was staring at him, a little crossly.

'Zak, be serious. Do you really think Dad would let us use that ship – millions of dollars' worth of space machine? He's not going to let us fly that thing, even if you are qualified now.'

Zak pulled a face. He hated to be beaten, but maybe he had been a little hasty. He knew how much the cruiser meant to their dad. He'd acquired it only the previous year after a long struggle to persuade the authorities to part with one of their older space-craft for his private use. Even though space travel was so common it was almost all on official lines. There couldn't have been more than a hundred private craft in the entire solar system – usually the privilege of presidents and princes – so they knew just how fortunate their father was. Zak had jokingly called it one of the perks of his dad's job, but he knew there was more to it than that. Roy Anderson had proved himself to be a valuable asset to the west's space exploration programme – a bold pioneer whose name would go down in history alongside great adventurers like Gagarin and Armstrong. Such a man had *earned* his right to buzz around the stars in his own machine.

And then Zak remembered that that was exactly what his famous father was doing at this very minute: buzzing around the stars.

'Hey!' he said, smiling. 'I forgot – Dad's away on a mission. He's not even around to ask. I'm sure he wouldn't mind us borrowing the cruiser while he's away.' He glanced at Becky. 'Besides, he needn't even know.'

'Zak, that's sneaky!' said Becky. 'Anyway, Mom'll never agree.'

Zak smiled. 'You leave Mom to me, Sis. I'm sure she won't stop us – now that I've got my wings.'

Eve's face clouded with doubt. 'I'm not sure about this, Zak. I mean, it doesn't seem right to use the cruiser, even if you can get your mum to agree.'

'Oh, *I* see,' said Zak, glancing across at Eve with one of his hurt looks. 'You don't trust me. That's what it is: you don't trust ol' Zak!'

'It isn't that,' she said softly, and she reached out her hand and laid it on top of Zak's. He drew his hand away smartly. He wished she wouldn't do things like that!

Eve went on, 'I do trust you, Zak, of course I do. It's just that— well, if your father found out . . .'

'I don't know what all the fuss is about,' said Tom, wearily. The others turned to him as he leaned his elbows on the table and cupped his chin in his hands. 'It seems to me the answer's dead simple.'

They stared at him, awaiting this great revelation.

'Go on, then,' urged Zak. 'Astound us all.'

'OK,' he chirped, straightening up. 'If you want to borrow your dad's space-cruiser, all you have to do is ask Captain Malone to join us for our holiday.'

Zak stared at him for a moment . . . then his eyes crinkled and the corners of his mouth curled up. 'Eureka! That's it! Good thinking, Tom.'

Tom glowed with pride for a second or two, then leaned back in his chair, arms folded like some great oracle.

'No trouble at all,' he declared. 'Now, any more problems?'

'Hang on,' said Eve, troubled. 'I don't get it.' She glanced first at Tom, then Zak. 'Would somebody please explain what's going on?' Then she noticed that even Becky was grinning.

'OK,' said the younger girl. 'It's neat. Captain Malone and our dad are old buddies. They've been flying together on and off for years. It's only these past few years he's been tutoring here at the training centre.'

At last a smile found its way on to Eve's lips. 'Oh, I get it—your dad wouldn't let Zak fly his cruiser, but he could hardly say no if an old friend asked him.'

'Especially as the cruiser is the very model they used to fly together,' added Zak, his grin almost meeting his ears.

A little cheer went up from the others and Zak pushed his chair away. 'Now, if you'll excuse me . . .'

11

He turned and headed for the exit, and as he went Eve called out after him, 'But, Zak – suppose he says no?'

The young pilot glanced over his shoulder.

'He won't,' he called brightly. 'He owes me a favour, remember! Just keep your fingers crossed that he doesn't have any other plans.'

Their last day on the moon was almost over when Captain Malone brought his answer. He appeared at the door of Tom and Zak's quarters just as they were about to head down to the canteen for their evening meal. When Zak saw the officer's face his heart sank. The instructor's normally cheerful smile was noticeably subdued.

'Oh . . .' said Zak, disappointed. 'It's no go. Am I right, sir?'

'Can I come in for a moment?' Malone replied.

Zak stood aside as his captain stepped into the room, and Tom, who had been lying on his bunk, jerked to his feet.

'At ease, Tom,' said the Captain, and then he turned to Zak. 'Sorry I couldn't give you an answer earlier, son, but there have been one or two difficulties.'

'Difficulties, sir?'

The officer nodded gravely. 'I haven't been able to raise your father.'

Zak said, 'I thought there was a hot-line, sir.'

'There is, but Mission Control are a bit sensitive about its use right now. Of course, I appreciate that he's operating an awful long way from home, being out there in uncharted space, but . . .'

'You mean they're not allowing personal calls,' Zak cut in.

The instructor hesitated. 'Look, let me give you the good news. I've spoken with your mother and she's quite happy about us using the space-cruiser. And yes, I'm prepared to fly with you.'

'Hey, that's great!' said Tom, grinning.

'Cut it!' barked Zak, irritably, and then he turned to Captain Malone. 'And the bad news?'

'Well, it's not that bad,' the officer replied. But his eyes did not reflect the smile in his voice. 'What I mean is, it might turn out to be more of a mission than a vacation.'

'I don't follow,' said Zak, anxious.

'Well, it's probably nothing to worry about, but . . .'

'*Please*, Captain – just tell me straight!' he implored. 'Something's happened to my father, hasn't it?'

'Well, that's just it,' Malone returned, struggling to take the sting out of his news. 'Nobody seems to *know* what's happened to him. Until two days ago his signal was coming through loud and clear, and then he . . . he just vanished.'

Five minutes later the girls arrived. Zak had contacted them on his wrist-phone and now they stood at the door bursting with questions.

'I don't understand,' said Becky, as she and Eve stepped into the boys' quarters. 'Dad couldn't have just disappeared. There's got to be a reason.'

'Yes,' said Eve, 'maybe he went out of range, or passed behind a planet somewhere.'

Captain Malone shook his head. 'We would have been tracking him pretty closely; we'd have known if he was likely to lose contact with us. Besides, he would have warned us if he thought we might lose his signal.'

'Then it must be a breakdown,' ventured Tom. 'Something's gone wrong with the system.' But he knew that was absurd – an outmoded idea – and the look he received from the others confirmed it.

Becky stood biting her lip. 'That means something must have happened that Dad wasn't expecting, like . . . like an explosion or something. Oh, I do hope he's all right!'

'I'd lay money on it,' the captain smiled. 'I know your dad too well – he's a survivor.'

'What are they doing to locate him, sir?' Zak asked.

'Everything they can, of course, but I guess at the moment that means relying heavily on sensoring equipment from the closest satellites. Your dad was operating way beyond the range of the patrol ships that escorted him to that space zone. Besides,' – and he hesitated – 'those ships have now been posted elsewhere.'

'How come?' said Zak. 'I mean, they can't just go off and leave Dad, not knowing what's happened to him . . . can they?'

Malone stood eyeing Zak for a moment, and not for the first time the youngster reminded him of Roy Anderson. It wasn't just the boy's features, like the jet-black hair and the determined eyes; it was as much the stance, and even the lilt of the voice. And he could have kicked himself for having to be the bearer of bad news.

'I'm afraid they had no choice, son. They received a request for help from our people on Delta-Nine.'

'The planet we discovered last month?' said Tom.

'That's it,' said Malone. 'The only trouble is, the Eastern Alliance has now laid claim to it, too.'

'But they can't do that,' Eve objected. 'We landed there first.'

'Try telling that to the Alliance,' said Malone. 'According to our surveys that planet's just loaded with mineral resources, and both east and west need those pretty desperately. We've both been waiting for a discovery like this for years, so there's no way the Alliance is going to sit by and watch us mine the place if they think they can muscle their way into a share of the booty.'

'But what's that got to do with Dad's escort ships?' asked Becky, perplexed.

The instructor glanced at her, and in the soft light of the boys' quarters he thought he saw her eyes glisten.

'Unfortunately, Becky, those ships were the nearest. Once it was established that there was nothing they could do to help locate your father's ship they were given clearance to respond to the emergency call.'

'In other words, Dad's been abandoned,' said Zak, angrily.

'No,' Malone replied – and there was just a hint of a smile on his face. 'I thought it was all agreed: we leave just as soon as we can climb aboard his space-cruiser. I've already notified Flight

14

Control – you know how they like prior notice of private craft using the space-lanes.' And he moved towards the door.

'But, Captain – what about the range problem?' said Zak, confused.

'What about it?' said Malone, and turned in the doorway, smiling.

'Well, if the escort ships were unable to go in search of Dad's craft, what hope do we have? Surely our range will be even more limited than theirs?'

'Could be,' grinned the instructor. 'But I never yet let a technical detail stand in the way of a challenge . . . and if you're Roy Anderson's son, neither will you.'

He grinned again and stepped into the corridor, but was then halted in his steps by the bleeper-alarm sounding on his wrist-unit. He looked at the unit and tapped one of its many tiny buttons. A small video-screen blinked into life. Looking out at him were the sharp features of Commodore Bryce, his immediate CO and the man who had to give clearance for their proposed flight. Malone's heart sank.

'Malone here, sir.'

'I've got your request for a civilian flight in front of me, Jack,' said the face. 'I'm afraid there's no chance of this – not now.'

The youngsters groaned out loud and Malone said, 'What do you mean, sir? What's the problem?'

'Haven't you heard?' said the officer. 'All leave has been cancelled. We're on standby for Red Alert. It looks like we're at war.'

At first the details were unclear but it came as no surprise to Captain Malone to learn that the crisis centred on Delta-Nine. He guessed that Starforce had called the Alliance's bluff, that shots had been exchanged, and that now the whole thing was escalating out of all control. He wasn't far wrong, but the how and why of it was not important; what mattered was that their plans were dashed. Unless . . .

'There's only one chance,' Malone told Zak. 'We appeal to the Controller direct.'

'C-Commander Drake?' gulped Tom.

'That's right. Don't look so worried, Son. Drake won't eat you! Now come on – we'll probably catch him in the operations centre.'

They took the travelator across the domed complex of Moon City, and as they entered the huge circular operations centre, its walls lined with row upon row of computer-banks and countless monitor screens, they spotted the Controller, deep in urgent conversation with his subordinate officers. Above their heads, a bank of screens showed what was happening on the distant Delta-Nine, and as the men talked they glanced up at the monitors and occasionally pointed at them. Their faces were grave.

'We'll never get near the Controller with this lot going on,' said Tom. 'They've got a proper war council brewing over there. He won't have time for us.' He really felt quite relieved.

But Captain Malone was already walking away from them. 'You wait here till I call you,' he said over his shoulder, and then headed straight for the stern-faced Controller, now breaking from the circle of men and striding away.

In a moment Malone had intercepted him, walking beside him for a few steps until he had the Controller's full attention. Then Commander Drake stopped and turned to face the Captain, his face grim.

The youngsters wished they could hear what the two men were saying, but whatever it was Tom doubted it would do any good. He remembered the Controller's lectures at the Academy – if they were anything to go by, it was highly unlikely that the old boy would approve of their plans.

'D'you remember those classes, Zak?' Tom groaned. 'He was a right ol' misery. I reckon if he smiled his face'd crack!'

'That's unkind,' said Eve. 'I don't suppose *you* would smile very much if you had his job, especially with a war threatening.' She paused, studying the Controller's tall, erect figure, his sharp features and hooded eyes. His hair, thinning on top, was silver. 'Anyway, he was always polite to me,' Eve went on. 'I think that hard exterior is just something he wears for the job. You can always tell by looking at people's eyes, you know. Commander Drake has got kind eyes, if you get a close look at them.'

Tom chuckled. 'Next you'll be telling us he's really a great big softy! Come off it!'

'Well, I heard he has sixteen grandchildren,' countered Eve, as though that finished any argument.

'Sixteen little monsters!' gasped Tom. 'No wonder he never smiles.'

Eve pulled a face – and landed a punch on Tom's shoulder.

'Cut it out, you two,' said Zak. 'Look, here comes Captain Malone. Stand by.'

Moments later they were filing into the Controller's plush office adjoining the operations room and lining up to attention on the deep-pile carpet in front of an enormous desk. Commander Drake was standing with his back to them, watching a monitor screen relaying pictures from the crisis zone, but then he turned, eyeing them coolly and returning

17

their trembling salute.

'At ease, everyone,' he snapped. 'Now, let me tell you straight – you have precisely four-and-a-half minutes before that screen over there flashes on and the President of the United States asks me for a full up-date on the Delta-Nine hostilities. So let's get down to business. Captain Malone here has already outlined your proposals. Normally, of course, what you did with your leave would be entirely your own concern; however, the present war situation has changed all that, as I'm sure you'll appreciate. We are now on Red Alert and you know what that means: all leave cancelled and no civilian flights of any kind.' He glanced at each of them in turn as disappointment shaded their faces. 'However, I . . .'

'May I say something, sir?' Zak cut in.

The Controller glared at the young pilot for a moment, irritated by his impudence. Starforce commanders were not used to being interrupted, especially by Grade III astronauts! But then the CO relented. 'What is it?'

'Well, sir,' Zak began, 'I realize that the present hostilities have made things very difficult, but I just wanted to say how disappointed I am that not more is being done to locate my father – that is, Roy Anderson, sir. I know he's only one man, and that one man is nothing compared with the millions who are now at risk through this war, but he matters a whole lot to me – and, sir, I'd like to request that in this case you waive the rules and permit us to at least *try* to locate my father.' He paused, swallowing hard. 'If – if that permission is refused, sir, I very much regret that I would have no alternative but to – to resign my commission.'

He glanced down, trembling, aware that the Controller's eyes were boring into him, and he stood there waiting for the inevitable explosion.

But it didn't come. Instead he heard Commander Drake grunt disapprovingly, then turn to Captain Malone. 'Just like his father,' he complained. 'Stubborn to the core.' But there was no anger in his voice and Zak looked up again.

18

Commander Drake was looking right at him – and for the first time Zak thought he knew what Eve had meant when she'd said the Controller had kind eyes.

'Do you realize I could have you discharged for speaking to me like that, Anderson?'

Zak said, 'Yes, sir.'

'Hm,' said the Controller. 'I thought as much.'

He turned to Eve, Becky and Tom. 'And what about you three? I suppose you're all in on this, are you?'

'Yes, sir,' they chorused, and Becky added, 'I'm Colonel Anderson's daughter, sir.'

Commander Drake's eyebrows arched in surprise. 'Are you indeed? Well, yes, of course – yes, you're very much like your father.'

Becky nodded. '*I'm* stubborn too, sir.'

The Controller tried unsuccessfully to stifle a small grin. 'Oh, of that I've no doubt, no doubt whatsoever.' Then he gave a cough, assumed his military demeanour once more, and went on.

'Now, as I was saying before I was interrupted' – he glanced at Zak – 'there are no civilian flights, and no leave. However, that does not mean I am ignoring your request that a rescue-ship be launched. Colonel Anderson is a highly valued member of this force and we believe in making every effort to locate him and to ensure his well-being.'

He paused, looking again at Zak, and in a slightly stiffer voice he went on, 'By the way, contrary to your comment that not enough is being done to find your father, I think you should know that we have diverted three of our prime deep-space satellites from their highly important roles in space communications and research to the task of locating your father's ship. That's approximately two hundred million dollars' worth of government hardware searching for one man. Believe me, if your father's ship is out there and can be tracked, that equipment will track it. The mystery, of course, is that none of our tracking stations has been able to pick up

19

anything that remotely resembles the scan-data of your father's ship. It appears that he has simply vanished from space. So let's not start assuming that little is being done, simply because we haven't yet sent out a search party.'

Zak coloured a little but resisted the urge to look down. 'I'm sorry, sir. I appreciate all that you're doing for Dad – I mean, Colonel Anderson.'

Commander Drake ignored the remark and went on, 'There *will* be a search party, and for this reason: for all we can achieve with our tracking stations, what we really need is to get another ship into the area where Colonel Anderson's craft was last reported.'

'Oh no,' thought Zak, 'they're sending someone else.' His heart sank, and he knew that the other three shared his feelings.

The Controller, meanwhile, had moved to a huge star map that occupied almost an entire wall of the office. His finger stabbed at the zone marked by a tiny replica of Colonel Anderson's spacecraft, the probe ship *Excalibur*.

'This is the Colonel's last known position – here, in the outer reaches of Quasar-Noma.' He turned and motioned for the others to gather round, and as they moved in behind him he went on, 'That, as you know, is unexplored territory – at least, it was until *Excalibur* entered that region three days ago. Now the reason for that mission – and this is A-classified information: absolutely top secret – was to investigate radio signals which appeared to emanate from that area. Signals, let me add, that were so faint they could only just be monitored by our most distant tracking station. But the message of those signals was unmistakable: SOS.'

Tom's eyes widened. 'Another ship in trouble, sir?'

'Possibly,' said the Controller, 'but if so, where did it come from? Certainly not from earth. Starforce has no hardware in that zone.'

'What about the Alliance?' suggested Eve.

The Controller shook his head. 'They've nothing that far

out – at least, not in this sector.'

'Could it be you're getting ghost-signals from one of the old explorer-craft?' said Zak. 'One of those unmanned probes sent up by the old NASA regime back last century?'

Commander Drake smiled. 'Good try. We thought of that one, but no – we checked them all out and in each case the trajectory was wrong. Besides, the power units of those things burned out years ago. There's always the chance of a freak burst of energy from them, of course, but nothing powerful enough to transmit a signal that we could receive. Anyway, as I said, the co-ordinates are wrong.' He paused, turning to look again at the star map. 'No, whatever is sending out those signals is something that did not originate from planet earth.'

'Gee,' breathed Zak, 'a distress call from another race of people!'

'So there *is* life on other planets!' exclaimed Eve. 'But where? Who?'

Commander Drake raised a hand to halt this flow of ideas. 'Let's keep our feet on the ground, shall we? We cannot assume anything until we have the hard evidence to back it up. For all we know we may have sent Roy Anderson on a wild goose-chase.' He paused, noting the anxiety on Zak's face. 'But that was a chance we felt we had to take. If there *is* intelligent life out there, the west must be the first to find it.'

The hooded eyes darkened and the Controller's voice became most grave. 'We daren't risk the possibility of the Alliance making the first contact with those from other worlds. At present we have the edge on the enemy and we mean to keep it that way. If there *are* other peoples out there beyond the stars we mean to have them on our side.'

'And that was Dad's mission?' asked Becky, her eyes bright with admiration for her father. 'Contacting strangers from another world? Wow!'

Commander Drake looked down at her, noticing again the family likeness. 'And now it's your mission,' he said, and glanced at each of them in turn, waiting for this to sink in.

It was too incredible. They couldn't grasp it straight away, and while their eyes widened and their hearts began to race, the Controller smiled to himself and lifted a file from his desk – a file marked 'Briefing: Priority–1'. He flipped it open and ran his eyes over the details set out beneath the Starforce insignia, noting the initials of Charles Fairburn, Commander-in-Chief, and the signature of the President of the United States flowing across the presidential seal.

Looking up, he exchanged a small smile with Captain Malone, then turned the open file round and set it down before the youngsters.

'There are your orders,' he said.

Zak gulped. 'You – you mean *we're* the search party? The *official* search party?'

'That's what it says,' confirmed the Controller. 'It specifically states that Pilot Zak Anderson is to command a Starforce ship whose mission is to locate *Excalibur*, to fulfil the assignment of that ship if it has not already been accomplished, and to make every effort to return Colonel Anderson to earth. Choice of co-pilot and crew to be at your discretion.'

'B-but why me?' stammered Zak, his legs suddenly feeling very wobbly.

'Don't ask me,' snapped the Controller. 'Ask Commander Fairburn.' And then he leaned forward and added, 'I don't know what you did to impress him, young man, but evidently he thinks you're pretty special.' He held out his hand. 'Congratulations.'

The youngsters glanced at one another, beaming, and suddenly they were bubbling over inside with relief and joy! In other circumstances they would have leapt up and down and hugged one another, letting out great whoops of laughter, but they thought better of it with the Controller of Operations watching them. Tom, however, did allow an exultant little hoot to escape, but that was quickly squashed by a dig in the ribs from Zak. Who could blame him, though? This was far more than they had ever hoped for or would have dared to believe!

They had come, hoping and praying for permission to take off on a personal quest, and here they were being commissioned by the greatest powers in the western world to fulfil that very role! Not only would they get their wish actually to go in search of Zak and Becky's father, but now they would do so with all the mighty resources of the Starforce system to back them up!

Zak turned to the Captain, both of them grinning from ear to ear.

'I – I don't know what to say, sir,' stumbled Zak. 'I mean, me being appointed commander of the ship and you being a captain an' all. Would you mind if – that is, are you still willing to come with us, sir?'

Malone beamed. 'You try stopping me, son!'

Zak gripped his hand, then turned to Commander Drake, and as he did so he was suddenly aware of the privilege and responsibility of the mission. An enormous sense of pride welled up inside him, and instinctively he found himself standing to attention and saluting the CO.

'Flying Officer Zak Anderson ready for duty, sir,' he said. 'When do we leave?'

Lift-off had been scheduled for 07.05 hours next morning – not long to wait. But to Zak and his crew it seemed an eternity! They were just itching to get moving and would have leapt into the cruiser and taken off that very minute if they'd been allowed. After all, that had been their original plan.

But things had changed – and how! They still would be using Colonel Anderson's space-cruiser, but, as Commander Drake pointed out, everything would now be done the Starforce way. That was good news indeed, especially for Zak. One of the things that had worried him about going in search of *Excalibur* on a private mission was that the space-cruiser had a far more limited range than the probe ship. He also knew that *Excalibur* was unique in the Starforce fleet: no other starship had yet been fitted with the revolutionary thermo-nuclear power unit that had enabled Roy Anderson to penetrate so deeply into hitherto unexplored space. But now that problem had been removed. The technicians had done their homework and calculated that the space-cruiser could quite easily be modified so that its old-style atom-powered engines could be replaced with the new thermo unit. That work had been in progress even as they had been speaking. In the morning they would blast off in the comforting assurance that their machine could now go as far and as fast as Roy Anderson's.

'Dad always complained that the cruiser was a bit sluggish in top gear,' Zak joked as the youngsters settled down to a meal that evening – their last meal on the moon for who-knew-how-long?

'That's all very well,' teased Tom, 'but who's going to foot the bill? After all, it's your dad's machine. I can just see it now – Colonel Anderson checking his accounts one morning and getting the shock of his life: "To supplying and fitting new space engines: $1,000,000"!'

They had laughed a good deal over that, but more because of the pre-flight nerves than the joke itself. None of them cared to admit just how tense they were feeling about the mission, but inevitably the subject came up and Eve confessed to having butterflies in her tummy!

'Butterflies?' scoffed Tom, who always liked to go one better than the girls. 'I feel as if I've got *space-rockets* chasing around inside me!'

'Oh, your butterflies *would* have to be jet-propelled!' sneered Becky. 'That's *just* like a boy.'

'What about you, Zak?' asked Eve, and Zak felt a funny tingle as she touched his hand.

'Oh, er – I'm all right,' he gulped, and suddenly thought his collar was too tight. 'Er, more coffee, anyone?'

After the meal they went to the video-phones and spoke with their parents back on earth before heading down to the briefing-room for an hour's session with the Mission Controller. Then they stopped off in the engineering dock to take a look at the cruiser before turning in. There was a great deal of activity going on, with a score of technicians fussing around the great machine and a clutch of officials standing on the giant wing comparing notes and shouting instructions. At the rear there stood a towering gantry from which the new power unit was slowly being lowered into position, and all around the cruiser stood the supply vehicles from which loads were being removed and taken aboard.

Zak had never seen the machine looking so good. Beneath the dazzling arc-lamps her plutonium-steel panels shone like silver, and the newly-affixed Starforce insignia stood out boldly on the tail-fin.

'Gosh, she's a real beauty!' said Eve, in awe. 'Like – like a great shining bird.'

'Best looking ship Starforce ever had!' declared Tom.

'Dad said the cruiser was years ahead of its time when it was first commissioned into service,' said Zak, his face glowing with pride. 'And it still is, now it's got the new engines. Why, I bet this could outrun anything in space – even *Excalibur*! Come on, let's have a look inside.'

Captain Malone was on the flight deck and they spent a long time talking about their various responsibilities during the mission and familiarizing themselves with the equipment they would be using. Then they poked their heads into the living quarters, snatched a glance at the cargo hold, and went back down the steps and headed for their sleep-units. The Mission Controller had requested that they be in bed by 22.30 hours and that time had just sounded on their wrist-alarms.

'Come on, we'd better hurry,' said Zak, and within five minutes they were each in their separate quarters, lying back ready for sleep. But by now the adrenalin was really flowing and none of them could seem to relax, so the medics came and gave them something to help them unwind. And as they drifted off, slipping comfortably into that other, distant world, each of them knew a gentle and pleasant excitement ... and they dreamed of stars, and the silver bird, and the great, great adventure.

'All systems are go! Commencing launch procedure.'

It was 07.05 hours precisely. Zak paused and took a deep breath. This was it.

'Hold tight, everyone. Ignition on – engines one, two and three.'

The three explosions became one and the ship shuddered momentarily. Then they were moving, slowly at first, but suddenly an enormous burst of power threw them back in their seats. The silver machine, its wings retracted for lift-off, leapt upwards, vaulting out of the underground launch bay and slicing into the lunar morning, gobbling up the miles and leaving Moon City's sprawling network of gently glowing domes far, far behind.

'A nice, clean getaway,' said the Mission Controller's voice. 'You're looking good.'

Zak grinned to himself. 'Thank you, Mission Control.' His eyes flitted expertly across the control console spread out before him, his keen mind absorbing the vital information that flashed gently from the dials and screens. Everything was functioning in perfect harmony, as expected.

Starforce technology, as everyone knew, was totally trust-worthy. The only uncertain factor about the flight was an external one: the threatening war with the Alliance. That had worried them and they had told the Mission Controller so. He had replied that if there was any risk of attack the launch would be delayed; and anyway, they would have a squadron of Strike Jets – Starforce's crack fighting machines – to escort them as far as Mars. There the SJs would be relieved by a battle-cruiser which would shadow them to the orbital path of Neptune. A second battle-cruiser would then take over, giving them cover to the edge of Quasar-Noma, the limit of its range and the point at which the escort ships had had to leave *Excalibur*.

'From there on you'll be safe,' the Controller had assured them during the briefing session.

'Unless we meet what Colonel Anderson met,' countered Tom in his gloomy prophet-of-doom voice, and the others had rounded on him and stared him into silence.

But Zak knew his friend had a good point because the question of what had happened to his father lay at the back of his own mind. Sooner or later they would have to face it – but there was no point in facing it earlier than necessary. Zak had later said as much to Tom.

'Strike Jets launching now,' said the Controller's voice.

Captain Malone, sitting beside Zak, leaned forward and ran his fingers over a series of control-sensors. Immediately a

27

bank of screens blinked into life in front of them, and they had 360° vision around the ship. Of their own choice they had launched 'blind'.

'Thank you, Control,' said Zak. 'We have the SJs on visual.' He glanced back over his shoulder to where Eve sat at the communications console. 'Let's wish the squadron leader a good flight, Eve. Link us up.'

With the initial lift-off procedures completed they were at last able to relax a little, and then they had time to gaze up at the screens and watch as the dangling coloured ball that was planet earth grew smaller by the second.

It was not a new sight to them, of course, but this time it was different: this time they were plunging into the unknown, and this time the solar system was at war. The news they feared had come through one morning like a cold hand on the neck: the Alliance had declared all-out space war. There was no turning back. What if the fighting spread to earth? With this question hanging over them their thoughts raced to their families and friends. Zak and Becky sat worrying about their mother back in Abilene, Texas, while Tom and Eve fretted for their families in England. Britain, being such a close ally of the United States, would almost certainly be drawn into any conflict with the Alliance. In fact the Starforce base in Suffolk probably would be one of the first to be attacked, being among the closest to Alliance borders.

'I feel awful, leaving Mum and Dad at a time like this,' said Eve. 'It's like running away. It seems awfully unfair of us.'

None of the other youngsters knew what to say to that, but Captain Malone turned in his chair, smiling reassuringly.

'They won't think you're running away. Believe me, they'll be proud of you – proud to know that you're part of Starforce and that the force is fighting for peace.'

Eve grimaced. 'What good is peace if there's no world left to enjoy it in?'

Even Jack Malone couldn't answer that one, and he turned away, remembering the last war – one that had claimed the lives of millions, including his own family. All of that had been in the name of peace, too.

Zak glanced round at his anxious crew and determined to change the subject.

'Mars, here we come!' he crowed, and as he enthused about the journey ahead of them all questions of war faded from their minds and their thoughts rushed ahead to the fantastic route that had been programmed for them.

Mars, Jupiter, Saturn, Uranus – they would enjoy spectacular, close-up views of all these planets before they swung off into the Milky Way and the mysterious Quasar-Noma.

But of course the crew's enjoyment had been the last thing in the strategists' minds when they had planned the route; it was strictly functional. In less dangerous times a more direct passage would have been chosen, but now they had to contend with the risk of attack by the Alliance. Journeying out past the planets meant that, if necessary, they could call on the many Starforce bases located along that trajectory. The major outposts were sited on Mars and Pluto, but there were also space stations strung out between all the planets and along their orbital paths, as well as Starforce bases on three of Saturn's moons. If assistance became necessary, Mission Control was confident that fighting machines from one or other of those bases would be able to get them out of trouble. Unless, of course, those ships were already engaged in some other conflict with the enemy. The regular reports they received from Control indicated that the space war was spreading fast.

'I do hope we're not attacked,' said Becky. 'I'd hate anything to prevent us from finding Dad.'

'Don't worry,' Tom told her, 'the Alliance won't try anything funny with a whole squadron of SJs protecting us. And even if they did attack they'd be sorry. We'd turn their fighters into scrap metal in no time!'

As it turned out, the flight to Mars went without incident and they settled down to enjoy the journey, only becoming anxious when the Strike Jets peeled away and there was a delay before the battle-cruiser *Orion* joined them. Such distractions were not unwelcome, however, for with the ship flying almost entirely on automatic systems the crew's duties were minimal and the abundance of free time was the one thing the youngsters found it difficult to cope with.

But they had been well catered for by the mission's planners. Stored on micro-tape in the cruiser's lounge were over 500 movies, 1,000 records, countless books and periodicals, and a vast variety of 'board' games. Each armchair had built-in video and audio equipment for individual programming, and there was also a communal system for when they wanted to enjoy one of the entertainments together.

For keeping fit there was the mini-gymnasium, and when their brains became dulled and they needed a little mental exercise there were endless puzzles and tests (aptitude, observation, reaction), all computer-programmed.

As the days slipped by they found themselves resorting more and more to these entertainments, for though they were travelling at phenomenal speeds the great emptiness of space robbed them of any significant impression of movement. If they hadn't known better they would have thought they were standing still. But everything changed when there was something to see!

'Asteroid belt ahead,' called Zak, and Tom and Becky came scooting on to the flight deck.

Spread out across their horizon, and stretching ahead as far as the eye could see, lay the vast ocean of asteroids – a familiar sight to commuters between Mars and Jupiter.

'Wow!' gasped Tom. 'Are we going to dodge our way through that? We're bound to crash – slow down!'

Malone laughed. 'What, and spoil the fun?' He turned and grinned at Tom. 'This is where we find out if our laser guidance system is as accurate as it's cracked up to be!'

Tom pulled a shocked face and clapped his hands to his eyes. 'I daren't look!' he cried, exaggerating to amuse the others.

'Nothing to worry about,' said the Captain. He turned to Zak, smiling. 'Your father and I used to have great fun weaving our way through here. We used to switch to manual controls and take it in turns to test our reactions. It was pretty hair-raising at times!' He glanced at the girls, who were looking anxious. 'It's all right, we won't be pulling any stunts like that on this run. Besides, the asteroids aren't as tightly packed as they appear from here; there's plenty of space in between!'

'They look really mysterious,' said Eve, 'like – like countless little planets searching for a resting-place.' She shivered suddenly. 'Ooh, it's quite eerie.'

'Well, you'd better get used to them,' said Zak. 'The belt's fifty million miles thick! They'll be keeping us company for a while.'

Eventually, though, the asteroids were behind them and ahead lay Jupiter, the gigantic striped ball that dwarfed every other planet in the solar system.

'It's incredible,' said Becky. 'To think that our earth would fit inside Jupiter thirteen hundred times. That's some planet!'

'Look, there's the Starforce space station,' said Zak. 'D'you see it, Eve? It's just coming into view.'

'I'll call them up,' said the girl. 'I rather wish we could stop off and stretch our legs a bit. We've come so very, very far.' And as she said it she glanced up at the screens where planet earth now showed as just a bright star and even the sun was little more than a tiny white disc. 'I do hope everyone's all right at home,' she murmured.

4

Time slid by and the space-cruiser plunged deeper and deeper into the eternal blackness. Jupiter lay far behind them, and waiting for them now was Saturn, the brightly-ringed planet with its nine moons: a glorious technicolour spectacle which awed the five of them into utter silence. This breath-taking view was reputed to be the most beautiful in the whole of the solar system, and it kept them marvelling for hours on end.

But soon Saturn too was just a memory, and before they knew it Uranus loomed ahead, almost 2,000 million miles from home!

To these young astronauts, of course, the distance meant nothing. They had grown up in a world which had already conquered its own solar system. The real challenge was the galaxy itself and beyond: the mysterious hidden places – like Quasar-Noma! One day, soon . . .

Meanwhile, on and on they went, slicing through the eternal void, boring deep into the dark chasms of outer space, each day no different from the one before or the one to come, apart perhaps from the occasional passing of a trade vessel or Starforce patrol. They saw nothing of the fighting that was now reported to be raging across the solar system, but Control kept them up to date on all developments. Thankfully it looked as if earth was going to escape.

This was greeted with cheers on the flight deck, but somehow the news was strangely muted by the fact that their home planet was no longer visible. They were now close to making the Neptune rendezvous and from there even the sun was but a bright dot.

'It's a peculiar feeling,' said Eve, 'now that dear old earth is out of sight.'

'Just wait till we intersect Pluto's orbit,' Malone told her. 'From there you won't even be able to distinguish the sun: it'll be just another twinkling star among thousands of millions!'

'Gee, I hope I won't get earth-sick,' murmured Becky.

Tom chuckled. 'Personally I can't wait to get out into the galaxy. Once we're rid of our doddery old escort we'll be able to put our foot down – full power, all engines. All stops out. Fantastic!'

Becky glanced at him. 'As long as we don't forget why we're here.' And there was just enough reproach in her voice to turn Tom's mind to other things.

The nearer they drew to their destination the more anxious Becky seemed to become, and Zak mentioned this to her as the pair of them began preparing their meal in the galley one evening.

'I'm sorry,' she said, unable to meet Zak's eyes. 'It – it's just the waiting. Sometimes it's unbearable, not knowing what's happened to Dad. Some days I feel full of hope, certain that he's safe and that we're going to find him. And other days . . .' She looked up at her brother, her eyes faintly moist. 'Do *you* think we'll find him, Zak? Oh, do say we will!'

He gripped her shoulder and smiled gently into her dark eyes. 'Listen, Sis, that isn't any half-cooked astronaut out there – that's Roy Anderson! And this isn't just a bunch of kooky kids shooting through space – it's *us*! Us and Eve, and Tom. And with Captain Malone that's a winning combination, right?'

The young girl nodded, blinking back a tear.

'You *bet* we'll find Dad,' Zak told her. 'We won't stop looking till we do!'

Good ol' Zak – she could always count on him to pick her up when she was down, and as they soared on, rocketing past Pluto's orbit and out of the solar system, then plunging deep into the galaxy beyond, his cheerful face and bright words became her own guiding star. When the doubts came swarming round and the blackness threatened to engulf her, she determined to set her sights on her brother's smile and to fix her bearings by his shining eyes. That made her feel so much better. Good ol' Zak!

But the day came when even the irrepressible Zak lost his smile.

The battle-cruiser which had been shadowing them since Neptune's orbit had long since turned back and they were on their own again, hurtling deep into the mysterious Quasar-Noma, barely a day's journey from where Colonel Anderson had disappeared. For a week now they had been sending out a continuous signal, hoping and longing for a response from *Excalibur*, but no reply ever came. The only signals that reached them were those of the mysterious and distant distress call that Roy Anderson had been sent to investigate. At first, of course, they had wondered whether that incessant SOS was from *Excalibur*, but Mission Control had checked it out and assured them that the signals were from no earth craft; they were the same bleeps that Colonel Anderson had been trying to track down.

'But it doesn't make sense,' protested Eve. 'If it's not an earth ship that's in trouble, why are they using *our* distress call? It's just too impossible to believe that another race of people in another part of the universe just happen to have devised the same SOS code as ourselves.'

'Well, if they're a superior race,' argued Tom, 'the chances are they've been observing earth's quaint old ways for years. They would certainly be familiar with our call-signs.'

'Yes, but if they're superior,' Becky chipped in, 'they would hardly waste their time signalling *us* for help. By their standards it's probably taken us an age to fly this far – I bet they could do the journey in a couple of hours ... minutes, even! Who knows what their technology is like? So they're hardly going to call us up. They'd probably all be dead by the time we reached them.'

'Have you considered it might be a trap?' said Zak – and Eve shivered as an icy ripple shot up her spine.

'Don't say that!' she trembled. 'You'll give me the creeps!'

'Yes, that's horrible,' said Becky. 'I can't bear to think of Dad being lured into some terrible danger.'

'Well, maybe ...'

'Maybe you guys should be keeping your eyes on the screens,' cut in Malone, a little irritated by all the speculation. 'Come and take a look. There's something out there.'

They quickly moved in around the Captain and stood staring up at the velvety blackness that filled their horizon.

'But all I can see are stars,' said Tom.

Malone shook his head. 'Look there,' he said, pointing. 'That's no star – it's getting bigger and brighter all the time.'

'Another ship?' said Eve, mystified.

'Oh, please let it be *Excalibur*!' blurted Becky. 'Please!'

Zak turned to Tom. 'Let's get a read-out on it – find out exactly what it is.'

'Aye-aye,' said the boy, returning to his post. 'Laser-sensors scanning now.'

Within seconds the invisible laser beams had reached the curious light and a complete analysis was being fed back to the space-cruiser and played out on a screen above the scanners.

'Doesn't make sense,' grumbled Tom, scratching his head. 'It doesn't have any sort of material structure at all.'

'What about the light source?' questioned Zak. 'What's the breakdown on that?'

Tom looked up, baffled. 'It doesn't have one. At least, our scanners can't identify any sort of metabolism. It – it's as if it's there, but it isn't. Crazy!'

'It's there all right,' said Malone. 'And it's growing by the second!' He glanced round at Tom. 'What's the range?'

'Just under 1,000 millitons.'

Zak turned to Eve, his mind racing. 'What about those

35

distress signals? Give us bearing and range – fast!'

Eve slipped to her console, her eyes flashing across the instrument readings.

'Bearing three-nine-green – range 1,200 millitons.'

'Eureka!' cried Zak, slapping the arm of his chair. 'That's it!'

'That's what?' chorused the girls.

Zak turned to them, beaming. 'Don't you realize? That light, whatever it is, is the source of the distress call!'

'But what *is* it?' asked Becky.

'I don't know. But don't you see? It might lead us to *Excalibur* and Dad.'

'It's some sort of cosmic phenomenon,' said Malone, checking Tom's scan data. 'It has no form as such. It's just a mass of energy. And it's big! Miles wide and – well, so deep the instruments can't even measure it.'

'But is it dangerous?' pleaded Becky. 'I mean – are we going to vanish just like Dad?'

There was fear in the young girl's eyes – a fear that now touched each one of them. Zak turned and laid his hand on his sister's shoulder, smiling gently.

'Well, I guess pretty soon we're going to find that out.' He glanced round at the others. 'Positions, everyone. Eve, contact Control and brief them on the situation. Tell them we're moving in.'

The Captain peered up at the screens again. 'I don't think we need worry about that,' he said dryly. 'Whatever it is, it's coming to us!'

And their breath was caught away as they realized how quickly the glaring ball of light was now rushing towards them.

'Reverse engines!' shouted Zak in alarm. 'We're pulling away!'

But Tom's reply sent a chill shooting through them. 'We can't! That thing's sucking us in. There's a gravitational field – massively powerful! Our engines are useless to resist!'

'Give it all you've got!' barked Zak. 'Full power!'

The great light filled the forward screens now – a vast, glaring light that was almost upon them.

Tom threw the engines into reverse and immediately heard them screaming as they fought against the incredible force dragging them forward.

'It's useless!' he cried. 'We're overloading the system! She won't last, Zak!'

Moments later the strange light was all around them and so dazzlingly bright they had to shut down the screens. The tortured engines protested even more fiercely, sending great angry shudders throughout the craft.

'For pity's sake!' yelled Tom. 'More of this and you won't have a ship left! I warn you, Zak, the engines won't . . .'

Ker-boom! An enormous blast rocked the space-cruiser, tossing them from their seats and dashing them to the floor. The cabin lights flickered and faded and darkness engulfed them. Silence stole through the ship and before anyone could speak they were moving forward, slowly at first, but then faster and faster.

'Oh, Zak!' cried Eve, but there was only a groan in response – and suddenly the ship was tumbling forward, tumbling and spinning through the mysterious corridors of unknown space. Down they went – down and down, hurtling faster and faster, turning over and over, their heads spinning madly.

And then, one by one, they slid into unconsciousness . . . and knew no more.

'Do come and look,' said Eve. 'It really is the most beautiful sight!'

She had been the first to waken and now stood beside Zak's empty seat staring up at the screens. To her surprise she felt perfectly well after her frightening ordeal – not even a trace of a headache!

Tom picked himself up, rubbing his elbow and yawning.

'I feel like I slept for a thousand years!' he chuckled as he came and stood beside the girl. Then he blinked hard, squinting up at the view on the screens. 'Hey! Where are we?' he demanded. 'And what's happened to the others?'

'They'll be all right,' Eve assured him. 'There's no harm done. But just look where we are!'

Tom blinked again. 'Why, we're in low orbit over some planet or other and – hey! I can see mountains and fields and the sun shining on a sparkling river.' He glanced at Eve and wondered whether he was still dreaming. 'Here, where are we? What's going on?'

Eve smiled at him, then turned to gaze at the view again.

'I don't know,' she said, and her eyes were dancing with delight. 'But did you ever, ever see such a beautiful world!'

5

Before long the others came to and got to their feet, reacting to the view with mixed feelings. While Eve seemed to have accepted and welcomed the lovely world that lay below them without question, Zak was disorientated and Captain Malone simply felt uneasy. Becky said she wasn't at all sure what to think, while Tom confessed to being totally and utterly baffled!

'It's like planet earth – only it isn't,' was how he finally summed up the beautiful scenes passing slowly before their eyes.

'Yes,' said Becky, 'all the scenic beauty of earth is here, but – well, it's somehow been rearranged!'

Eve shook her head. 'No, it's more than that,' she insisted, and by this time they were studying the planet in close-up through the cameras' high-magnification lenses. 'This is somehow much better than earth. Like earth must have been before it was –'

'Spoilt?' ventured Zak.

'Spoilt!' agreed Eve. 'That's exactly right!'

'Oh, you mean like Paradise!' offered Tom, and Eve's eyes lighted up with approval.

'Paradise!' she breathed.

Captain Malone coughed impatiently and the youngsters glanced round as he slipped into his seat at the control console, smiling with amusement.

'I, er – I hate to be the one to mention it, but in case no one's noticed, we're drifting around your so-called Paradise without power, and if I'm not mistaken' – he glanced at the instrument readings – 'we're also gradually losing height.'

39

'Oh, er – yes,' spluttered Zak, sliding into his seat and trying to cover his embarrassment. 'Er, positions, everyone. Stand by!'

But, as they quickly discovered, there was nothing to stand by *for*. The explosion in the engines had put the motors out of commission, and inspection revealed that repairing the damage would take several hours.

'We just don't have that sort of time,' Malone told them when he and Zak returned to the flight deck. 'As I said, we're losing height by the minute.' He glanced soberly at each of the youngsters in turn. 'I don't like it, but we're going to have to put down on the planet.'

'Why, that's wonderful!' said Eve, still caught up in the beauty of the strange world.

Malone stared at her. 'I hope you're right – but personally I like to know a little more about an alien world before setting foot on it.'

'Yes,' said Zak, 'for all we know the place might be overrun by savages.'

'Cannibals, even,' volunteered Tom in his usual helpful manner.

'Tom!' scolded Malone.

'Sorry,' said the boy, thrusting his hands into his pockets. And with an irritable glance at Zak he mumbled, 'It's isn't *my* fault we're in this mess.'

'Oh, it's *my* fault, is it?' Zak sprang at him. 'That's right, blame me for everything!'

'Well, I told you the engines would burn out, but you wouldn't listen. Like Commander Drake said, you're stubborn, Zak!'

'Why, you . . .'

'Hold it, hold it,' cut in Malone. 'No one's to blame here, Tom. The gravitational field around that light would have sucked us in with or without our engines running. We were powerless to resist and you know it.'

'He's right, Tom,' said Becky, gently squeezing the boy's

arm. 'Anyway, what matters is that we're here and we're going to have to make the best of it. Besides' – and she turned to look up at the screens – 'maybe Dad is here too ... somewhere.'

'I – I never thought of that,' said Eve, her eyes wide. 'Of course! *Excalibur* may have been swallowed up by that strange light, too!' She turned to Malone. 'But whatever *was* that dazzling thing? I mean – where are we? All I remember is the lights going out and us rushing through space, tumbling and turning, going down and down. Wherever are we now? I do hope we're not lost.'

Captain Malone eyed her seriously for a moment, then went and stood looking down at the control console, stroking his chin in deep thought.

'I've been thinking on that since I glimpsed these readings when I first woke up,' he said. 'I'm afraid I don't much like the conclusions I've come to.' He tapped the instrument readings panel with his finger. 'See here, this distance recorder has run right off the clock, and that's – well, impossible.'

'What d'you mean?' asked Zak.

The Captain turned to face him. 'Well, if we're to believe the reading, it means we've travelled something in excess of ten times the distance we covered from earth to Quasar-Noma.'

'Why, that *is* impossible,' said Tom.

Malone nodded. 'Especially as we made the journey in just a few hours.'

Becky said, 'How do you figure that, sir? I checked my watch when I came to and it had stopped at the time the engines cut out. So had the clock on the console.'

The others quickly checked their own watches and Malone said, 'That's right, and I think you'll find that every time-piece on the ship stopped at exactly the same moment.'

'Hey, you're right,' said Zak. 'Then how come you know how long we've been travelling? We could have been

41

unconscious for days.'

The Captain laughed. 'A foolproof method,' he said, rubbing his chin again. 'I'd shaved about an hour before we encountered the light and I reckon there's half a day's growth of beard there now.'

'Then the instruments must be up the creek,' protested Tom. 'We couldn't have travelled half-way across the universe in a few hours.'

'Quite right,' said Malone. 'Unless we hit a space-warp.'

Four mouths fell open and eight eyes stared.

'Why, that's it!' blurted Zak. 'That would explain everything!'

'How come?' queried Eve. 'I don't know that I fully understand this space-warp business.'

'It's like the Captain said before,' Zak explained. 'The light was a cosmic phenomenon – a freak occurrence. There are millions of them, happening all the time, all over the universe. This one just happened to be a – a sort of galactic doorway.'

Eve blinked in surprise. 'A doorway? You mean, opening on to a sort of space corridor connecting distant galaxies?'

Zak nodded vigorously, and Tom said, 'A cosmic short-cut!'

'Well, it's real enough,' said Malone. 'We don't need to fully understand it to know that. But exactly where we are and how we managed to end up in orbit round this planet is anyone's guess.'

'Where do the SOS signals fit in, sir?' asked Becky. 'How could radio signals be coming out of a – what did you call it, Zak? – a galactic doorway?'

The Captain curled an arm round the girl's shoulders. 'Now there you've got me, young lady.' He glanced up at the screens and the beautiful view, and the youngsters' eyes followed. 'Maybe the answer to that one lies down there somewhere.'

The silent ship drifted on along its orbital path, slowly falling to ground while the crew made preparation for the touch-down. Most important of all was to locate a suitable landing site. Given the right conditions Malone knew they could glide the space-cruiser down, but what worried him was having enough room. Without the retro-rockets to brake their landing speed the momentum of the machine would hurl them along the ground for miles before they came to rest.

With the help of the laser-sensors and computers, however, a suitable site should not be difficult to locate ... providing it existed.

Zak and Malone concentrated on this problem while Tom busied himself with scanning the planet's surface for the other information that was vital to them: was the air breathable? And what sort of temperatures would they find down there? All the evidence of an environment capable of supporting human life seemed to be present, but one of the fundamental lessons learned by young astronauts was that in the alien world of space you do not believe everything you see.

Eve's responsibility during this anxious time was more straightforward – to attempt to contact Mission Control and to inform them of their predicament. A simple enough procedure normally, but an impossibility when the transmitter and receiver are separated by thousands upon thousands of galaxies. If only Eve had realized how very far from home they were!

Becky's duty was even less demanding – making the coffee! But the question burning in her mind at that moment was very similar to Eve's thoughts: even if they should find her father, how could they ever be sure of being able to return to earth? Surely they would need to go back through the space-warp something so ... unpredictable.

But suddenly Zak's voice rang through the ship and their various thoughts were lost in a chilling mixture of wonder and fear.

'A city!' he cried. 'Look, everyone – on the horizon! A city that glints like gold!'

They all gathered round the screens. There, away in the distance, stood a vast and magnificent city, sparkling in the planet's sunshine like a royal jewel.

The nearer they drew the more awed they became. Zak had instinctively known that this was a city, and yet it was quite unlike any group of buildings they had ever seen. No architect could have conceived such beautiful and diverse designs and made them fit together so perfectly, and where in the universe was there a building material that shone so brilliantly!

'I – I do believe I must be dreaming,' murmured Eve. 'Why, I have never, ever seen such a wonderful sight. It – it's simply heavenly!'

'Just look at the way that little cluster of towers reaches into the sky,' breathed Becky. 'Like – like the fingers of a huge hand. Fantastic!'

'Who ever could live in such a place?' muttered Tom. 'I hope they're friendly!'

'Oh, they are,' said Eve. 'Don't ask me how, but I just know they are! Friendly people, gentle and peaceful.'

'I get that feeling too,' said Zak, glancing at the others. 'I can't explain it, but somehow I've got such a good feeling about this place. I really don't think we have a thing to worry about.'

Malone glanced at the instrument readings. 'I sure hope you're right, because ...'

He never finished. Away in the distance the rounded tips of the tall finger-like buildings suddenly opened up like flower-petals in the sun and from each of the fingers a shining sphere shot out into the sky.

The five of them stared, mesmerized.

Amazingly, each of the spheres stopped at exactly the same height from the ground – about the same height as the space-cruiser – and before Zak could even blurt out 'Spacecraft!'

the curious shining balls, each about a metre in diameter, were hovering round the ship. No one had seen the spheres travel the few miles from the city: one moment they were stationary over the finger-buildings, the next they were round the cruiser. Tom's mouth fell open. How did *any* machine move that fast? What sort of technology did these people have? And why was the space-cruiser being surrounded?

'R-raise defence shields!' he cried, forgetting there was no power. But he needn't have worried, for a moment later the radio-screen blinked on and smiling out at them was the warm and friendly face of an old man with flowing white hair and the brightest eyes they had ever seen.

'Please don't be alarmed, earth friends,' he said in a soft, soothing voice. 'No harm will come to you here. We have been expecting you and you are warmly welcome. My name is Quintay and I am head of our family here on Terran. It is my privilege to greet you all in the name of The Maker.'

Zak stared up at the gentle face, speechless.

At last Malone spoke up for them all. 'Er, we – we bring you greetings from our planet, sir – planet earth – which you seem to know of already. We come on a peace mission, seeking a friend lost in space.' He paused, wondering how to explain the embarrassment of being without power, but Eve was eager to speak to this friendly-looking being from another world and she leapt in at the first opportunity.

'Sir, we are very happy to be here, but we have a little problem . . .'

'I know,' said Quintay, smiling. 'Your engines are not functioning. But that is a small matter and is why five of our machines are surrounding you. While we have been talking the machines have been attending to your technical problems. I think you will find that your engines will fire now.' And as he finished speaking the strange spheres disappeared.

Zak stared at Tom, who suddenly felt he had to sit down. How could those overgrown ball-bearings diagnose and repair extensive damage to planet earth's most advanced thermo-nuclear engines in a matter of minutes, just by hovering round the cruiser? Was this some kind of weird joke?

Zak was equally sceptical but he couldn't resist programming the computers for the ignition procedure.

'That's impossible!' he spluttered, when he heard the engines blast into life. And the old man laughed.

'All things are possible to those who believe,' he said, and Eve had the strangest feeling she had heard those words somewhere before.

Malone was watching the instrument readings, which told him that the engines were running perfectly, and he couldn't help grinning to himself. Looking up at the screen he said, 'Well, I don't know how you did it, but – thanks.'

The old man chuckled. 'Think nothing of it. Now if you'll fly over the city you'll see our spaceport. I'll be there to greet you when you land.'

The smiling face vanished from the screen and they all looked at one another in astonishment. What an amazing beginning!

'Fancy them looking like us!' said Tom, who had quite expected to see a green monster with three heads . . . but was glad he hadn't!

'The technology!' said Malone, shaking his head in wonder. 'Incredible! Light years ahead of us!'

'And they speak the same language!' gasped Becky. 'It – it just doesn't seem possible!'

'There,' said Eve, 'I knew we had nothing to worry about. What a kind and lovely old man.' She turned and grinned at Zak. 'What did he call this planet – Terran? Yes, Terran. I think I'm going to like it here.

They flew in low over the city, feasting their eyes on the magnificent sights, their hearts warming to this wonderful new world. The metropolis, they discovered, was set amid the loveliest countryside any of them had ever seen – but rather than being an eyesore on the landscape, as were so

46

many of the high-rise cities on earth, this one blended perfectly with the natural world.

'It's as though it grew *out* of the land, rather than being plonked on top of it,' was Eve's observation.

'Mm,' agreed Becky, smiling fondly. 'It looks a little like a flower from up here, doesn't it – with the buildings sort of spreading outwards like petals.'

'Oh yes – and look, everything seems to centre on that beautiful park. Why, it must be miles wide! There's a lovely lake, too. And see that funny little round building right in the centre! I wonder what that could be?'

'Probably a bandstand,' volunteered Tom. 'But I don't see any chairs for the people.'

'Hey, look!' grinned Zak. 'There are some people waving at us! Aren't they friendly? You'd think they'd be scared stiff of a strange spacecraft roaring over their quiet city. Wow, what a place this must be!'

'Spaceport dead ahead,' said Malone, and Zak turned to the controls with a huge grin.

'Commence landing procedure. Sit tight, everyone.'

They stepped out of the space-cruiser, unable to believe their eyes. Travelling towards them from the spaceport buildings was quite the strangest vehicle they had ever seen – like a gigantic, transparent egg – and seated inside, one behind the other, were four people, one of whom they recognized as the friendly old man.

'How ever does it move?' cried Zak. 'No wheels of any kind and yet it's travelling a good metre off the ground!'

'Must be some sort of hover machine,' suggested Tom, but as the strange 'egg-vehicle' drew near they could tell it w̲ₐₛ nothing so primitive, for there was no trace of any kind of power unit – and no sign of any controls, either.

But it was an even bigger surprise when the old man and his companions stepped out of the 'egg', straight through the 'shell', as though it wasn't really there. Yet it sounded firm enough when Zak gave it a discreet little tap with his knuckles. What other marvels did this strange planet hold, they wondered.

'Welcome, welcome!' beamed the old man, eagerly shaking hands with each of the five. 'It is an honour and a joy to have you here. Now please meet my family . . .' And one by one they were introduced to Quintay's wife, Shara, and their two youngest sons, Daffon and Briod.

'What strange names,' thought Eve, which was exactly Briod's thought when he was introduced to Zak, Tom, Becky . . . *most* peculiar!

Tom, meanwhile, was wondering how old the Terran boys were. They *looked* about their own age – teenagers – and yet Quintay and his wife were old enough to be their grandparents. Or were they? As they had already seen, things on Terran were not always quite what they appeared.

They stood there beside the space-cruiser for another few minutes, exchanging interplanetary small-talk until the old man suggested they drive back into the city for refreshments.

'Er, what about our spacecraft?' said Zak. 'Shouldn't we move it off the runway?'

'Oh, that won't be necessary,' replied Quintay. 'Our people will move it for you.'

'But hadn't we better show them how it works?'

They knew by the twinkle in the old man's eye that nothing of the sort would be necessary. As Tom later remarked, 'Anyone who can repair blown-out nuclear engines with a handful of giant ping-pong balls would hardly need to be told where the starter button was!'

The Terran people certainly had an astounding grasp of technology. And in his mind Captain Malone was piling up the questions he longed to ask. How, for example, could the strange egg-machine seat only four people on its way out to the space-cruiser, and nine on its way back? And that walk-through shell needed explaining, too.

But the questions on Zak and Becky's minds were even more pressing, and as their strange transport whisked them out of the spaceport and across the fields to the gleaming city, the young Andersons bombarded their hosts with one query after another.

Had the mysterious distress call been sent out by Terran, or by one of its spacecraft? Had they seen any sign of another earth craft, the probe ship *Excalibur*? Or a stranger dressed like themselves in Starforce uniform? And there were many other questions, all asking the same things in different words, and all receiving a negative reply.

'But we shall help you search for your father,' Quintay promised them, 'if you wish. At the very least we shall place our knowledge of the planet at your disposal and offer you any assistance we can.' He turned and smiled at Becky, his bright eyes somehow so reassuring. 'You can be sure of this, Becky – if your father *is* on Terran we shall help you find him.'

His wife turned to him. 'You must ask The Maker tonight, dear.'

'Yes, yes,' said the old man, nodding. 'The Maker will know for sure.'

Eve glanced at her hosts with curiosity, then looked round at Zak and Tom, both of whom shrugged their shoulders. Well, it seemed there was only one thing to do and that was ask.

'Excuse me, but who *is* The Maker you speak of?'

Quintay and Shara exchanged a look of surprise and even their sons raised their eyebrows. What! Did these earth people not know about The Maker? Were they clever enough to build spacecraft (agreed they were *primitive* spacecraft) and yet did not know the One who gave them breath and placed the stars in the sky? For a moment the old man was at a loss to know how to answer.

'Why, my dear,' he said at last, 'The Maker is the very centre of our world. Did you not know, he constructed the universe and set the planets in their orbits. He made everything that ever *was* made.'

'Look out, dear!' cried Shara as they zoomed into the city, narrowly missing another egg-machine coming the other way!

They all laughed with relief as Tom made a little joke about omelettes, and Quintay said, 'I always take that corner too fast. Now where was I?'

'You were telling us about The Maker,' Becky prompted.

'Oh yes. Well, what can I say? He's our Father, our Counsellor, our Friend – everything! Life itself. Without him we would merely exist.' He laughed shortly. 'And what an existence!' He turned to his wife. 'Can you imagine it, my dear, if The Maker never came to the garden again? Why, I'd prefer the sun to stop shining.'

'And you say he would know if *Excalibur* is here?' said Zak, hope rising in his voice.

'My dear boy,' smiled Quintay, 'The Maker knows everything!'

They moved on through the streets, peering at the strange and wonderful buildings and watching the people going to and fro. They really looked no different from earth people, thought Eve, except for their clothes. The styles and fashions were quite unlike anything on earth: literally out of this world! The colours, too, were sensational – 'like nothing on earth'!

What struck them most, however, was the look on people's faces. That too was unearthlike!

'Gee, everyone seems so happy here,' said Becky, putting into words what each of them felt. 'I don't believe I've seen one sad or troubled face.' And for a moment her thoughts flashed to planet earth . . . and the terrible space war they had left behind them.

Shara turned to her, puzzled. 'I'm sorry – what do you mean, "sad"?'

'And "troubled"?' added Daffon. 'We have no equivalent to those words in our language.'

The five friends looked at one another, bewildered.

'But you speak the same language as us!' Becky said blankly.

Quintay and his wife exchanged an amused glance, then with a chuckle the old man said, 'We don't, actually. My, what a coincidence that would be! No, you are hearing us in your native tongue, but in fact we are speaking our own language. On the other hand, you are speaking an earth language, but we are hearing you in Terranese.'

Malone glanced at Quintay, trying to decide whether the old fellow was teasing them. He certainly had a twinkle in his eye. But having already seen so many remarkable and unlikely things on this planet, the Captain thought almost anything must be possible!

'I know you find it difficult to believe,' Quintay went on, 'but if we weren't able to understand one another there would hardly have been any point in your being sent here. I said as much to The Maker and he told me he had already taken care of . . .'

'Just a minute,' Zak cut in. 'Did you say that we were *sent* here?'

'Why, yes,' replied the old man. 'I told you we'd been expecting you. Surely you didn't think you arrived here by accident?'

'Here we are,' called Briod as they turned another corner. Suddenly all their questions dried up as they looked in amazement at the extraordinary building in front of them. It was a single-storey structure of a most peculiar design, yet delightful to look at.

Briod turned in his seat, smiling. 'This is our home,' he told them.

'Look,' said Eve, 'it's right opposite the park we flew over.'

'The garden,' corrected Daffon. 'That's the garden.'

'It's beautiful!' breathed Becky.

'Do mind the kerb, dear,' said Shara.

'Of course,' Quintay responded. But as they turned off the roadway outside the strange house the egg-vehicle shook with a little bump and Quintay sang out, 'Sorry!'

Shara smiled at him with gentle reproach and Malone scratched his head in bewilderment. How did *that* happen when the vehicle was floating a metre from the ground!

But suddenly the thought was gone and he was shouting, 'Look out!' The house was only metres ahead and yet Quintay wasn't slowing down.

'Nothing to worry about,' called the old man – and as the five space travellers gasped in alarm and braced themselves for the crash they all passed through the wall and stopped in what they took to be Shara's lounge!

The Captain stared across at his hosts. 'W-wasn't that a solid wall?'

'Of course,' smiled Quintay.

Malone nodded, feeling a little wobbly. 'That's what I

thought,' he muttered.

'Wow! Just look at the view!' gasped Tom, who was the first out of the strange vehicle. An entire wall of the house was a huge picture-window looking out over what Daffon had called the garden – except that the 'window' was not made of anything so primitive as glass. In fact it appeared as if absolutely nothing stood between Tom and the view . . . until he tried to walk *through* the 'window' and bounced off it.

But that was a small wonder compared to the view itself.

'How do they do it?' gasped Zak. 'This is only a single-storey home . . .'

'. . . and yet we're looking down on the garden as though we were ten storeys up!' finished Eve, and one by one their mouths fell open. How on earth . . . ? But, of course, this *wasn't* planet earth.

'Do sit down,' said Shara. 'Refreshments are on the way.'

And what surprising refreshments they were: cups of tea and cakes, not so very different from what they were used to back on earth! But *how* . . . ?

'With the compliments of The Maker,' Quintay told them. 'He wanted you to feel at home.'

At the mention of The Maker Zak's thoughts flew to the questions that had been on his lips when they had arrived at the house. He sat looking across at the old man, troubled. Quintay did not miss a thing. 'What's on your mind, young man?'

'Lots of things, really,' Zak replied. 'For a start I'm puzzled by what you said about us being sent here. What did you mean?'

'I'm not sure I know the answer to that myself,' said the old man. 'All I can tell you is that we knew someone from planet earth was to visit us, and that you should be present at tomorrow's meeting of the People's Counsel. The Maker made that very clear.'

'May I ask what this People's Counsel is about?' asked Malone. 'Some sort of official meeting?'

Quintay nodded. 'Of a sort. Our community here is administered by the decisions of the Counsel. There are twelve of us who meet regularly to discuss the city's affairs and to share with one another what The Maker has been saying to us.'

'Does The Maker really talk to you?' asked Becky, who was fascinated by the very idea.

'Most assuredly,' came the reply. 'That is, he speaks to us within our spirit.' He turned and glanced fondly at the splendid view of the garden where the first tinge of dusk was settling around the trees. 'Morning and evening he speaks. In the garden. To everyone. Wonderful!'

'It will soon be time, too,' added Shara, her eyes gently shining.

'Oh good, can *we* come?' asked Tom, reaching for another cake.

And for the first time the old man's smile dissolved.

'I'm afraid that won't be possible.' He glanced at each one of his visitors. 'Now please don't be offended, and don't ask me for reasons, but I regret you are not allowed in the garden when The Maker is there.'

'Unless . . .' prompted Shara.

'Oh yes, forgive me, I almost forgot.' He shifted uneasily in his seat, as if not sure how to go on. 'Now I don't pretend to understand this,' he said, 'but my wife is quite correct, there is an exception to this rule. This is what The Maker told me to tell you: "Only he may enter who knows by name the Lamb."'

He fell silent, watching the five faces for some flicker of recognition, but all that met his eyes were five blank stares.

'Very well,' Quintay went on cheerfully, 'my family and I will go to the garden while you settle into your rooms and make yourselves at home. I think you'll find everything you need is there, but if not you've only to ask.' He stood up, smiling gently. 'We won't be long. You just sit there and finish your tea. Explore the house when you're ready and you'll soon find your rooms.'

'Er, Mr Quintay,' said Zak, not at all sure how to address an important member of another world, and he got to his feet to add weight to his question. 'You won't forget to ask The Maker about my father's ship? It's very important.'

'Of course it is,' Quintay smiled. 'No, I won't forget, and you'll have an answer, too. Don't you worry about a thing. Have some more cake and we'll be back before you know it.'

A few minutes later the five stood looking out over the beautiful garden, watching in wonder as people streamed in from every direction to walk among the trees and sit beside the brightly-coloured bushes and blooms. They came in ones and twos, in families, and in even bigger groups – hundreds of them, maybe thousands. It was impossible to know how many, for the garden stretched almost as far as the eye could see, with the distant, silhouetted buildings only just visible on the horizon.

Their earth minds found it a most peculiar arrangement that everyone in the city should come to the garden morning and evening to talk to someone they couldn't even see. And what a strange name – The Maker.

'He must be really special,' mused Becky. 'I wonder what he talks to them about.' And then a cloud came scudding into her thoughts and she felt a little sad. 'I wish we *were* allowed in the garden.'

Captain Malone smiled at her. 'Well, I guess there's a pretty good reason why we're not. The Maker doesn't sound like he'd keep us out unless it was really necessary.'

'No,' said Zak. 'Anyway, it wasn't as though The Maker didn't give us a chance. If we'd known the answer to that riddle we'd be over there now with Quintay and the others.'

'Yes, what *was* that riddle?' said Eve. 'Only he may enter who ...'

'... who knows by name the lamb,' finished Zak. 'I wonder who the lamb could be?'

'Or *what*,' said Tom. 'Animals aren't people.'

'Yes, but this one seems to have a name,' countered Becky, looking very puzzled. No one seemed to know what to say after that, so they stood there watching the dusk settle over the garden while the late sun bled glorious colours into the sky over the distant city buildings. Then Zak turned to the others.

'Come on, let's go and see what our rooms are like.'

'*If* we can find them,' chuckled Tom. 'I hope we don't have to walk through any walls.' And then he thought again. 'Or maybe I do!'

It was a great adventure, exploring such a strange house on such a strange planet, and they had fun peeking into the different rooms, marvelling at the odd-looking furniture, and discovering how things worked. The lighting system kept them amused for a long time, once they'd discovered that it operated in response to their thought-waves. If they *thought* it was too bright, the lights would dim to just the right level ... and the other way round. They also found that in the same way they could choose the *colour* of the lighting to suit their mood. But try as they might they could not locate the source of the illumination. There were no bulbs, not even concealed ones; the light was simply there! What surprises this world held for them!

But the biggest surprise of all came when Quintay and his family returned from the garden with their news. Zak was so excited he could hardly keep still as the old man told how he had enquired about the lost probe ship and its solitary occupant ... and how The Maker had assured him they would have the answer in the morning.

'But why can't we know now?' groaned Zak.

'Please tell us,' said Becky. 'Please! We're so worried about Dad.'

'I understand,' replied Quintay. 'But I'm afraid I simply don't know anything. Wait until the morning and then you'll know for sure.'

'But why can't we know now?' persisted Zak.

Quintay turned. 'Because,' he said patiently, 'The Maker wants to tell you himself. Tonight, while you sleep.'

It was such a vivid dream that Zak was not sure he had been asleep at all. Perhaps he had been out flying over the strange planet by night . . . except that it had been broad daylight and there was no flying machine of any kind – just him floating along and looking down, his eyes searching for any sign of *Excalibur*.

What he knew for certain was that The Maker had been as good as his word.

Moments later he was out of bed, waking Tom to tell him. Then Becky came bursting in, her face aglow as she sang out, 'Zak! Zak, I know where Dad is!'

'Me too!' whooped her brother, and they hugged each other and danced around the room, laughing and grinning . . . leaving poor Tom to wonder whether *he* was still dreaming!

'Come on,' beamed Zak. 'We must tell Quintay – and then we must get started right away!'

7

What fantastic news! At long last they knew where their father was – or at least they could describe the place, and Quintay was sure to know where to find it. Off they went, rushing through the house, laughing together and calling out for Quintay and his wife. They found them up and dressed and sitting at the family table, sipping a drink of some kind.

'Good morning to you! I take it you got your answer!' chuckled the old man. 'Now tell me what you saw.'

Zak couldn't get the words out quickly enough! 'Well, I was flying, sir, flying high and fast, zig-zagging between the mountains, and then there were miles and miles of fields, golden in the sun . . .'

'Yes, and there was a river,' Becky cut in. 'Wide and fast-running, and then more mountains, only smaller and somehow darker.' She glanced at Zak. Had he seen the same thing?

'That's right, and beyond those I started to fly lower and lower, until I was in some sort of valley with huge trees and dense, dark undergrowth. Then the trees thinned out around a rocky area – like a canyon – and there, down below, was *Excalibur*!'

'As if it had made a forced landing,' added Becky. 'But it was there, as clear as anything. I could even see the name on the tail-plane.'

'Why, that *is* good news!' said the old man. 'And was there any sign of your father?'

Zak shook his head. 'But I just know we can find him, once we've located his ship. Where is that place, Quintay? Tell us where it is and we'll head out there right away.'

The old fellow laughed. 'All right, I'll tell you where to find the place you've described, but it won't do you much good flying out there in that odd-looking machine of yours.'

'Why not? I know it's not as advanced as anything you've got here, but . . .'

'Oh, it isn't that,' Quintay smiled. 'But in your own craft you'll need a landing strip, and in that region there's simply no area that's suitable.'

'Couldn't we put down in the canyon?' asked Becky. 'It seemed miles long and it was certainly wide enough.'

The old man shook his head. 'That canyon is strewn with boulders that would tear your craft to shreds. No, you'll need a machine that's able to land vertically and precisely at a chosen spot. But that's no problem.' He turned to his wife. 'What do you think, dear – get Micha to fly them out there?'

Shara nodded. 'I can't think of anyone better. But what about the Counsel meeting?'

'Oh, my word!' exclaimed Quintay. 'In all this excitement I quite forgot.' He turned to Zak – but then Captain Malone and the others appeared. 'Ah, good morning. I trust you all slept well.'

'Like a log,' grinned Tom – and for the first time their host was aware of a language problem.

'Oh, how do logs sleep? Come to that, why do they need to?'

They all laughed. 'Sorry,' said Tom, 'it's just one of our sayings. It means we couldn't have slept better!'

'That's good,' smiled Quintay, 'because it looks as if you're going to have a busy day.'

'We've already heard,' said Malone. And with a teasing glance at Zak he said, 'Somebody woke us up to let us know the good news! In fact, I dare say they woke the whole house!'

'Oh, it would take more than that to wake *my* two boys,' said Shara. 'They're a couple of sleepy-heads.'

'It's time they were up, anyway,' remarked her husband. 'They can drive our guests to the spaceport.' He turned to Captain Malone. 'We were just saying that you'll need a machine that can land you in the rocky valley. So we're going to ask a friend to fly you there. But this is what I wanted to say' – and he paused, glancing at each of the five in turn – 'by all means go off on your search, but please remember that The Maker requires your presence at our People's Counsel this afternoon. I have no idea why, but I do know that this is of the utmost importance. Besides, I'd like one of you to make a little speech to the Counsel, bringing greetings from your own planet and so forth. It isn't every day we have people dropping in from another world! So do try to be back in good time. You can always resume your search after the meeting.'

The youngsters nodded.

'Micha will see that they're back in time,' said Shara. '*He* won't want to be late for the meeting.'

'Excellent,' said Quintay with satisfaction. 'Now I expect you'd like to bathe and get dressed. I think you know where everything is.'

'And what about some breakfast before you leave?' added Shara.

'Thank you, but no,' said Zak. 'We're really much too excited to eat.'

'Hey, speak for yourself!' protested Tom.

'Another few minutes won't make much difference, Zak,' said Malone.

'Quite right,' agreed the old man. 'Anyway, it will take a little while for me to arrange your transport.'

'And the meal's ready and waiting for you,' added Shara. 'The Maker gave me one of your recipes – a most peculiar dish it seemed to me, but he assured me you would approve.' And with a twinkle in her eye she went on, 'Do flapjacks and maple syrup sound good?'

They took off about forty minutes later in what Tom called 'a flying goldfish bowl' – a large, transparent sphere which seemed capable of all sorts of aeronautical tricks, as demonstrated by its pilot, the man called Micha. He was friendly-looking, with yellow curly hair and those same bright eyes. Everyone quickly took to him. At first they thought he was about the same age as Captain Malone. Yet at times he seemed so much younger . . . or older. Another Terran mystery! Apparently he had helped build the strange machine now whisking them over the wonderful countryside towards the distant mountains, and he was quick to answer their questions about the amazing Terran technology. But he seemed keener still to tell them about the planet itself, and about Quintay and Shara, the dear old couple the five were growing to love.

'They're kind,' said Eve. 'And very loving. No wonder they were chosen as leaders of your people, Micha.'

The pilot glanced at her. 'Oh, but they've always been head of the family here, right from the beginning, before even the city was here. That was the way The Maker planned it.'

The girl's eyes flashed with a gentle excitement. 'Tell us about it, Micha – about the beginning of things.' And she glanced back at the gloriously shining buildings now far behind them. 'Tell us about The Maker, and the city.'

'Yes,' said Tom, 'how *did* the city begin?'

'Very well,' smiled the pilot. 'As much as I am permitted to tell.' He shifted in his seat as he settled down to his story. 'It began long, long ago when The Maker planted a garden here and decided to make a man and a woman to enjoy all that he had created. But most of all he made them so that he could enjoy their company, and they his. He also set himself a task and decided to allow the man and his wife to help him.'

'Let me guess,' said Becky. 'The task was to build the city, right?'

Micha nodded. 'The way he went about it was this: in the middle of the garden The Maker provided great knowledge and learning, from the most elementary scientific principles – the natural laws which he decreed – to the development of the ultimate technology. This knowledge was stored in thousands of small cubes – transparent, glowing cubes, just the right size and weight for a man to hold in his hand. And by holding the cubes, one at a time, for as long as he felt he needed it, the knowledge passed into the man's understanding.' He paused, glancing at his eager listeners.

They were so engrossed they hardly noticed the beautiful snow-capped mountains passing them by far below.

'That first man was Quintay,' Micha continued. 'His name means "son of the earth", for that is how he was formed, from the dust of the ground. Well, the more Quintay learned, the more of The Maker's plan was revealed to him. Together they would build a city.'

'What, just one man?' queried Malone. 'One man to build a city?'

Micha smiled. 'No, not just one man, Captain – one man plus The Maker. That *is* a considerable difference! And of course later on there were his children.'

'But all that work!' gasped Tom.

The pilot laughed. 'Oh, I know what you're thinking, but it wasn't back-breaking drudgery.' He glanced at the boy. 'Forgive me for saying so, but you can't view it in the same way as you would the building of a city on earth. This was a supreme joy.'

'But where did the materials come from?' asked Zak. 'And the technical equipment?'

'The Maker provided everything that was needed,' was the pilot's simple reply. 'All he asked of Quintay was his co-operation.'

'But it'd take a lifetime to build a place like that,' protested Tom.

'Oh, several,' said Micha. 'At least, several *earth* life-spans, but no such thing exists here. There is no death on Terran.'

The five friends glanced at one another in bewilderment. No death! Could this be true?

'But clearly there is an ageing process,' reasoned Malone. 'We've seen children, young people – all ages through to older people like Quintay and Shara. Surely one day their bodies will simply wear out and they'll die?'

The pilot shook his head. 'No, what you mistake for an ageing process is the development of maturity. Quintay and Shara have reached a marvellous maturity in their relationship with The Maker. They won't change any more.'

Eve stared at Micha wide-eyed. Perhaps it was all a dream. If so, in her dream she said, 'You mean that Quintay and Shara will remain here for ever?'

The pilot smiled. 'Oh no. One day, when The Maker decides, he will take them home to be with himself.'

'Oh, how lovely!' breathed Eve.

Micha turned and beamed at her. 'Nothing is more lovely than being with The Maker,' he said.

They flew on over the golden fields and the rushing river. Then the second range of mountains loomed up and they began their descent. There was so much to see – and so much to think about. What an amazing planet this was! A fabulous city that shone like gold . . . curious 'egg-vehicles' that grew to fit their passengers . . . solid walls that people could walk through . . . ground-floor windows that gave you a tenth-floor view . . . gentle people with shining eyes who would never die . . . and in the centre of it all the one they called The Maker – the wonderful, invisible friend who met with his people morning and evening in the beautiful garden that he himself had planted – the one, Quintay said, who knew everything there was to know.

As they flashed along in yet another of the planet's wonders – the 'flying goldfish-bowl' – Zak hoped and longed that they would find that to be true. The dream had been so vivid, and Quintay had been so sure. 'In the morning you'll know,' he had said, and they had believed him. Surely The Maker wouldn't let them down now! And though he would not have admitted it, Zak suddenly found himself reaching out in his spirit to speak to the invisible one for himself. 'Please let Dad be safe,' he was saying. 'Please, Maker. Please!' Whether or not he expected any sort of answer he didn't know, but there *was* one. Not in words, but an answer all the same. A strange and wonderful peace stilled all his anxious thoughts – like gentle waves washing the seashore and smoothing the sand. Somehow, instinctively, he knew that everything would be all right.

'Look!' cried Becky. 'That's the valley down there, straight ahead!'

Zak confirmed it. Yes, there were those towering trees and the dense, dark undergrowth. That was exactly what they had seen in the dream, and now they were here!

'The canyon lies just beyond,' said Zak. 'There, it's coming into view now! *Excalibur*, here we come!'

But though they flew the length of that rocky place there was no sign of the probe ship, nor any evidence that it had been there. Oh the agony of that disappointment! Had it been *just* a dream after all? Or could The Maker have got it wrong? Surely not. Still hopeful, they flew back down the canyon . . . but again there was no sign of the earth ship.

'Perhaps there's *another* valley,' ventured Tom. 'Another canyon. There could be dozens of them.'

But Micha knew the area well. This feature of the landscape was unique. That was how Quintay had been able to identify the location so readily. 'I'm afraid there are no more canyons,' Micha told them. 'If your father's ship ever landed in such a place this side of the mountains, it was here.'

They flew back up the canyon again, more slowly this time and much lower, but still there was nothing.

Becky felt crushed. 'It *must* be the wrong valley,' she said desperately. 'It *must* be.'

Micha turned to her, smiling gently. 'It's the right place, Becky.' And there was such conviction in his voice that she believed him. But she was still confused.

'Then why can't we see the ship? *Excalibur* was so clear in the dream. Why can't we see it now we're here?'

'Well, there can be only one answer to that,' said the pilot.

Zak thought about it for a moment. 'You mean that Dad's ship *was* here, but now it's gone?' And suddenly he felt that incredible peace within him again, and he knew that he had hit on the right answer. 'Yes. Yes, that's it! *Excalibur* was here but now she – she's been moved!'

'Come off it,' muttered Tom. 'Look at the size of those rocks down there. Like Quintay said, they'd tear a ship apart – especially if it crash-landed. Even if your dad had managed to put *Excalibur* down in one piece there's just no room for him to take off again. You know he'd need a good quarter-mile. It just doesn't add up.'

Micha slowed the craft to a stop – a complete stop, there in the air, about fifty metres from the ground – and turned to face the younger boy. His bright eyes bored deep into Tom's. 'Sometimes there is an explanation the mind could never conceive of.' He smiled. 'Will you trust me, Tom? This *is* the place in Zak's dream. Why don't we go down and have a look round? We may well find some clue that can't be seen from up here.'

Tom flushed slightly. He didn't know why, but he somehow felt self-conscious whenever Micha looked at him with those shining eyes. It was as though the pilot could see right inside him. But that was impossible . . . wasn't it?

'OK,' he agreed, and found that his voice was so squeaky that he had to clear his throat. 'Let's go down – but it'll take a lot to convince me that *Excalibur* was ever here.'

Micha just smiled and turned to Zak. 'About how far into the canyon was the ship in your dream?'

Zak looked at Becky. 'Half a mile?'

'No more,' said the girl. 'It's difficult to say, Micha.'

'All right, we'll fly back again and you tell me when to stop. Then we'll touch down and search the area.'

So off they went again with everyone looking down into that rocky place where boulders and stones lay strewn across the ground as though aimlessly tossed into the canyon by some unseen giant hand. It was strange, thought Eve, but there was something about the canyon that contrasted starkly with everything else she had seen of the planet's surface. It was not so much the appearance of the place, though, for the canyon possessed a raw beauty all of its own; it was more the feel of it. It was somehow lonely and desolate . . . eerie, even. There was certainly something eerie about the idea of a spacecraft landing here and then being removed without taking off. What could cause such a thing to happen? Some mighty and mysterious power, perhaps. And as Becky called out for Micha to stop the ship and they descended slowly to the canyon floor, Eve shivered uncontrollably. She did not like this place and she found herself almost wishing they would find no trace of *Excalibur* so that they could hurry away.

Moments later there was a tiny bump as the craft touched down and then they were climbing out through the solid shell on to the stony ground. To either side of them, beyond the scattered boulders and stones, the great rugged walls of the canyon climbed away into the sky, towering high above them. The rock formations were quite striking in their appearance and Captain Malone would gladly have spent the day climbing about the place. Geology fascinated him and as he stared around he found himself comparing the canyon with formations he had once studied in the rock hills of Mars.

Becky, however, had noticed something else.

'Listen,' she said, gazing round. 'Can you hear it – that awful silence?'

Zak scowled at her. 'Don't be silly. You're imagining things.'

'No, she's not,' retorted Eve. 'It's creepy. It's *too* quiet.' And she wrapped her arms around herself and shivered again.

Tom sniggered to himself, creeping up behind the blonde girl with his hands raised like the cartoon ghosts he'd seen. 'Silent as a t-o-o-o-o-m-b!' he wailed – and Eve shot away from him, squealing.

'Cut it out,' snapped Zak. 'We've got work to do.'

But Eve was really frightened and Micha went softly to her with a reassuring smile. 'Are you all right, Eve?'

'It's this place,' she said, feeling slightly foolish. 'It – it's somehow chilling.'

He nodded. 'I can feel it too. But don't be alarmed. There really isn't anything to be worried about.'

'Come on, everyone,' called Zak. 'Let's get moving. Shall we split up, or what?'

'We ought to have some sort of plan,' suggested Malone, 'so that we cover the area thoroughly. How about if you four go that way, towards the valley, and Micha and I search over here, up the canyon?'

'But what are we looking for?' asked Tom with a trace more impatience than he meant to reveal. He really was sceptical of the whole exercise.

'What do you think?' came Zak's curt reply. 'Anything that will give us a clue to *Excalibur* having been here. Now come on – we haven't got all day.'

And so they began their search, working across the canyon and back again, slowly moving outwards from the spot where Zak and Becky had thought their father's ship had been in that vivid dream. Eagerly their eyes scoured the ground for any tell-tale clue that would confirm that *Excalibur* had been here – except for Tom, who quickly grew bored and took to kicking the dusk with the toe of his boot. This was a waste of time, he told himself, regardless of what Micha said. It stood to reason: a craft of that size crash-landing would leave its mark, and even if that wild idea about the ship somehow being mysteriously removed were true, the marks would still be there. They would have been visible from the air, too. Unless, of course, somebody had co-vered them up. But why should anyone do that! The whole thing was ridiculous.

By the time they had reached the end of the canyon, where the rocks thinned out and the greenery of the valley began, the others were beginning to wonder if Tom was right. There was simply no sign that a spacecraft had landed in this remote and lonely place. But, as Zak pointed out, that would mean The Maker had got it wrong – and that was the one factor that drove him on. It was irrational to think this way, of course. It went against everything he had been taught at Space Training School. But his instinct told him that The Maker wouldn't lie. He would not accept defeat.

'We're not giving up yet,' he told the others as they paused at the end of the canyon. 'There just *has* to be a clue somewhere.'

Tom groaned and took a swinging kick at the dust – which turned out to be the best thing he'd done all morning!

Zak had been about to lose his temper with Tom when suddenly he stopped, his eyes drawn to the piece of ground just thumped by Tom's boot. Both boys looked down, then at each other, open-mouthed.

A moment later Zak was on his knees, digging furiously with both hands, sending great showers of dust into the air. His mind raced, his heart thumped. Yes, there *was* something there – something that was definitely not Terran soil.

'It's metal!' he cried, scooping away the dust.

'And big!' added Tom, squatting to lend a hand.

Then, as they exposed the edges of the object, they suddenly knew what it was – and they didn't know whether to laugh or cry.

It was a piece of metal, roughly triangular in shape, with one jagged edge where it had been ripped away from a larger structure.

'It's part of a fin!' gasped Becky. 'That means Dad *did* crash!'

Zak glanced at her anxiously. 'Not necessarily,' he said, with more hope than he felt. 'This could be off any ship; it doesn't have to be *Excalibur*.'

But they all knew he was clutching at the wind. Terran craft were not built of this type of material. And as the boys finally eased their find from the ground and turned it over they caught their breath.

There was no mistaking it. How could they mistake the Starforce insignia?

'But why should anyone want to bury it?' protested Becky, tears welling in her eyes.

'You usually bury evidence,' said Tom flatly. And for once he wasn't trying to be funny.

Eve shivered again and glanced over her shoulder. 'I knew I was right,' she muttered. 'There's something very wrong about this place. I didn't like it here from the beginning. There's something wrong . . . something evil.'

The boys got to their feet looking intently at her. Why *was* she so frightened?

'Relax,' said Zak. 'There's really nothing to be scared of. Besides, we're all together. We can handle anything that comes, you know that.'

The girl nodded, smiling weakly, and Becky looped her arm through Eve's.

'I don't particularly like it here, either,' the younger girl confessed, 'but we daren't leave now, not just as we've hit on the first real clue to what happened to Dad.'

Eve turned and smiled at her. 'I know. It's stupid of me to be so nervous, but it's just a feeling I've got. At first I didn't know what it was – I thought it was just the place itself. But now that we've found this fin I realize it's more than that.'

They all stared hard at Eve.

'What are you driving at?' said Zak.

She glared at him. How could he be so dim?

'Don't you see? I thought this planet was so wonderful with the shining city and all the friendly people, but that was only the good side.'

'What *are* you rattling on about?' Tom scoffed. 'You're beginning to sound ridiculous, Eve. Terran's a great place . . .'

'I know it is,' the girl cut in, 'but that doesn't alter what I feel.' And she squatted down, running her fingers over the smooth surface of the broken fin. 'Don't ask me how I know, but finding this has confirmed it.'

'Confirmed what?' spluttered Tom, who was quickly losing patience.

The girl looked up, her blonde hair framing a very worried face.

'Isn't it obvious? Someone on Terran doesn't want us to find Colonel Anderson. Someone here is our enemy.'

An enemy on this wonderful planet? The very idea was absurd. But before anyone had time to say as much they saw Captain Malone and Micha hurrying towards them, dodging between the boulders and jumping the little rocks strewn across their path.

'What is it?' called the Captain. 'Have you found something?'

Zak snatched up the fin and lifted it high above his head, the Starforce insignia facing the two men. Malone's eyes flashed and he cried out, 'Jupiter! The dream was true!'

'We found it right here, sir,' said Becky as the men picked their way through the last of the rocks. She brushed an escaping tear from her cheek. 'It was buried.'

'Buried?' retorted the Captain. 'But who in space would want to bury the thing?'

Zak handed him the jagged fin. 'That's what we'd like to know. It seems we were never meant to find it; it was pretty well hidden.'

'Well, I've said what *I* think,' said Eve, turning away, 'but nobody wants to believe me.'

Malone glanced at her. 'And what *do* you think, Eve?'

'Oh, it's all right,' she replied, sounding very hurt. 'They all think I'm bananas.'

'We don't,' insisted Becky. 'That's not fair. It's just that we don't have any reason to agree with you.'

'Then why was that fin buried, and why ...'

'Hang on a minute,' Malone cut in. 'Would you mind letting us in on this discussion? Who thinks what?'

'Well, *we* don't think anything yet,' Zak explained. 'But

Eve's got this idea that we've an enemy here on Terran. She thinks *he* buried it – whoever "he" is.'

'I didn't say it was a he,' the girl protested.

'All right,' grated Zak. 'He, she or it – what difference does it make!'

'It's utter rubbish,' scoffed Tom.

Eve turned on him. 'Then how did that fin get buried? Go on – tell me!'

'It's a good question, Tom,' said Malone, and he was pleased to see Eve back off and relax a little. But Tom was ready with an answer.

'Maybe Colonel Anderson buried it himself. Perhaps he did crash-land here and the fin got torn off by the rocks. There was no way he could fix it, so he decided to leave it. He buried it to cover his tracks. There!' And he folded his arms and stared round in smug defiance.

Zak shook his head. 'Tom, that's a lousy explanation and you know it! It's even worse than Eve's. You yourself said Dad wouldn't have been able to take off from here with all these boulders everywhere. And even if he had he couldn't have covered the tracks he would have made getting airborne again.'

'Well, maybe he took off, landed somewhere else and then came back to –'

'Tom!' scolded Malone. 'Why don't you just admit that we don't *know* how or why this fin was buried.'

'*Or* who buried it,' added Eve. 'And that brings us back to *my* theory!'

There was a moment's pause while everyone considered this, but before anyone could comment Micha spoke up. 'Do you think we could continue this debate on the way back? We really ought to be making a move.'

'Oh, do we *have* to leave right now?' groaned Becky.

'Yes, just when it seems we're really getting somewhere,' said Zak.

The pilot smiled. 'I know how you must feel, but that

meeting *is* important. Besides, as Quintay said, you can come back later.'

'But what about Dad?' persisted Becky. 'What if he's lying hurt somewhere? Anything could have happened to him. *Please*, Micha, let us stay just a little longer. I'm sure the meeting will keep.'

Micha smiled again, but this time there was a strange intensity about his eyes, and the girl knew he would not be swayed.

'I understand your reluctance to leave here, all of you. Right now you must be feeling that nothing in the entire universe matters so much as finding Colonel Anderson. But I would ask you to believe me when I tell you that there *are* more important things, and one of them is the outcome of this afternoon's People's Counsel.'

Malone turned to face him. 'Is it really that critical that we're there at the meeting, Micha? Y'know, we've come an awful long way to find Roy Anderson, and . . .'

The pilot raised his hand. 'Perhaps it will help if you remember that you did not simply *come* to Terran – you were brought, and for a specific purpose. If you honour the One who brought you here by fulfilling that purpose I am sure that he will honour you in your own business.'

'You're talking about The Maker, right?'

Micha nodded, pleased that they understood.

Malone turned to Zak. 'This is your mission, son – it's your decision.'

The boy hesitated, suddenly aware of that extraordinary peace once more . . . and he just knew they had to leave.

'Come on,' he said, crooking the fin under his arm. 'The Maker won't let us down. I'm going to trust *him* to help us find Dad.' And he was away, chasing down the canyon towards Micha's flying machine. 'After all,' he called back, 'he was right about *Excalibur*!'

Flying high above the planet through a cloudless sky the five earth travellers sat in silence, gazing down at the breath-taking scenery, their heads whirling with questions. One of these questions stood out above all the others, and when eventually one of them spoke it was inevitable that they should ask about the meeting.

'What will you be discussing?' enquired Malone, hoping to learn just why it was so essential for them to attend.

'The cubes,' came Micha's short and baffling reply.

'What about them?' asked Eve, who felt much better now that they had left the canyon. 'I thought you finished with the cubes once the city had been built.'

Micha gave a short laugh. 'Goodness, no! That would mean we'd nothing more to learn.' He tapped the see-through shell of the spherical craft with his knuckles. 'You didn't think this was the ultimate technology, surely?'

'Sure beats anything we have on earth!' grinned Malone.

'Maybe, but don't think we've arrived just because our technology is that much more advanced. I can assure you we've a long way to go before we reach perfection. The more we learn the more changes we make to our machines and to the city itself.'

'It's a very strange way to learn, if you don't mind me saying so,' said Zak.

'Better than sitting through lectures at the Academy!' chortled Tom. 'Boy, I wish *I* could have learned everything just by holding those strange cube things in my hand.' Then he turned to Micha. 'Will we see the cubes this afternoon? I really would like to.'

'You certainly will,' said the pilot. 'As I said, we shall be discussing them – or rather, one in particular.'

'Which one is that?' asked Becky. 'Or aren't you allowed to say?'

'Oh, it's no secret,' Micha told her. 'You see, when The Maker placed all the knowledge in the garden he told Quintay that there was only one cube he must not touch. All the others were his to hold whenever he was ready for the

73

knowledge within them. But not this special one; that was *never* to be touched for it contained a very different type of knowledge that would do the people more harm than good. And to make sure that the people never forgot, The Maker set it apart from all the others and caused it to glow more brightly.'

'How very odd,' murmured Becky – but she was not remarking about the cubes. She sat gazing down as they passed over the rushing river, very distant, as though in a dream. 'As you were talking, Micha, I had the strange idea that I'd heard all this before somewhere.'

The pilot turned to her, his bright eyes smiling. 'Perhaps you had. Why not think about it? You might remember something very important.'

Malone stared at the yellow-haired man, intrigued. He couldn't make head or tail of all the things he was hearing! At last he said, 'So what's the problem? If The Maker has told you never to touch this special cube, why do you need to discuss it?'

'Ah, if only every one of our twelve thought like that!' said Micha – and then everything fitted into place.

'Oh, I see,' said the Captain, nodding. 'There are some members of the Counsel who think you ought to go ahead and hold the cube. Disregard The Maker's instructions and grab the forbidden knowledge!'

'That's it,' said the pilot, a little wearily. 'At first there was only one who thought that way, but he has a smooth tongue and, sadly, others have listened to him. Gradually he has won the support of another five of our members.'

'Gee, that means your Counsel is split right down the middle,' said Becky.

Micha nodded. 'One more vote and he'll have a majority. Then Terran is in a dangerous position.'

'But would it really be so awful if you held that cube?' argued Tom. 'I know you think the knowledge it contains might do you more harm than good, but you never know, it might be the best thing that ever happened to Terran. I mean, are you *sure* The Maker told you not to touch it?'

'Oh yes, I'm quite sure,' answered Micha firmly. 'Besides, The Maker created us, and he knows what's best for us.'

There was no answer to that.

They flew in over the golden fields, dropping down through the mountains until the peaks towered above them. The loveliness of the views filled their eyes, and they gasped as their pilot chased low down the scenic valleys and zig-zagged through snow-brushed mountain gorges. As they shot up over a hill and began bearing down towards the distant city Micha called back to Zak, 'Care to take the controls for a while? I won't be able to return to the canyon with you this afternoon, so you'd better get used to her now.'

Zak didn't need any coaxing – but how could he fly the thing from the back seat?

'No problem,' said Micha, and he turned to extend a hand towards the boy. Opening his fist he revealed a short, chunky silver rod lying in his palm. 'Take it,' he said. 'Hold it loosely in your fist until you want to make any adjustments to speed, direction or whatever. Then simply apply a little pressure and *think* your instructions. The craft will respond immediately. If you want to cancel out any instructions for any reason simply tap the top of the bar with your thumb; then reprogramme. OK?'

'Er – sure,' said Zak, taking the silver rod but mentally reeling at the idea of controlling a spacecraft with thought-waves. 'I sure hope I don't think the wrong manoeuvres!'

'Don't worry,' Micha assured him, 'the one thing you can't do under this system is crash. There's a sensoring device that will automatically adjust your programme if for any reason you misjudge things. Or you can simply let the machine do *all* the work, if you wish. Just programme your destination and you can sit back and enjoy the ride.' He laughed. 'But that's the lazy way – and besides, it's no fun. It's much better

75

to operate it manually. Once you get used to the system you can test all your flying skills, and you can do it without the risk of an accident.'

'That's really neat,' remarked Captain Malone. 'Are all your machines operated in this way? We rode to and from the spaceport in a sort of egg-shaped vehicle.'

'And we nearly had a smash-up with another one!' added Tom. 'Almost ended up as scrambled eggs all over the road!'

Micha laughed. 'I know – but I assure you, Quintay's driving is a lot better than it used to be. D'you know, he once dented a dozen vehicles in as many months! But we soon put a stop to that!'

'How was that?' asked Zak. 'Did they ban him from driving for a while?'

Micha grinned. 'No, we just developed a material that wouldn't dent! If he hit anything after that, which he still does from time to time, the dents would just pop out and he wouldn't even be left with a scratch.'

Zak turned to Becky, grinning. 'Pity Mom didn't have one of those machines when she was learning to drive, eh, Sis?'

'Would've saved Dad a fortune in repair bills!' she declared, laughing.

'I take it the egg-vehicles don't yet have the anti-crash mechanism, then?' ventured Malone.

'Not yet,' Micha told him. 'But it'll come. There's a whole lot of development to be undertaken, but we're in no hurry. Time is one thing we have plenty of.' And then a shadow fell across his eyes and his smile faded. 'At least, that's the plan. Things could change after today.'

Malone turned to him, wondering just why that meeting was so important. 'Are we going to be in good time?'

Micha nodded. 'In plenty of time, Captain. I was asked not to tell you until we were on our way back, but Quintay has arranged a surprise lunch for you in the garden, down by the lake. He wanted you all to meet the members of the Counsel informally before the meeting begins.'

The youngsters exchanged approving glances. Those flap-jacks were nothing but a memory now, so lunch would be welcome!

'A picnic in the garden!' exclaimed Eve. 'That sounds lovely. Full power, Zak! I can't wait to meet everyone.'

'I'll just take it steady, if you don't mind,' said the boy. 'I want to get the hang of this control system if I'm going to have to fly us out to the canyon this afternoon.'

'You're doing fine,' Micha assured him. 'Just take her down slowly as we approach the garden.'

'But I thought we were going to land at the spaceport,' said Zak.

'Normally, of course, we would,' the pilot explained, 'but we've been given special clearance to land beside the lake, alongside the lunch tables!' He laughed. 'Quintay thought that would be a nice dramatic touch: visitors from outer space dropping in out of the sky!'

'Er, d'you think this visitor from outer space could clean up before she drops in?' asked Becky, inspecting her hands. 'I'm awful grubby after scrambling about on those rocks.'

'Don't worry, it's all been taken care of,' Micha smiled. 'Shara will be there and she'll show you to all the facilities you need.'

Tom said, 'What about her sons – what are their names? Daffon and Briod, isn't it? Will they be there?'

'They may well be,' replied the pilot. 'Yes, I expect they'll be around somewhere, if they've finished their studies for the day.' He turned to face Tom. 'Do you get on well with them?'

'They're good fun,' said Tom. 'We had a good laugh with them on the way out to the spaceport this morning. I bet they're a riot at parties!'

'How many children do Quintay and Shara have?' asked Becky. 'I know Daffon and Briod are the youngest. I suppose all the others have left home? Is it a big family?'

Micha smiled. 'Oh, it's a big family all right! Do you remember me telling you that Quintay was the first person on

77

Terran? Well, Shara was the second.'

'Shara – what a lovely name,' said Eve. 'It's beautiful. Did The Maker name her?'

'No, Quintay gave her that name. It means "mother of all living" – which she is, of course.'

Becky's eyes widened. 'You mean that Quintay and Shara are literally the parents of everyone on Terran?'

Micha chuckled. 'I said it was a big family! Yes, they had children who grew up to have their own children, who grew up to have more children . . . and so it goes on. I think there's something like thirty generations in all.' He turned quickly to Zak. 'Take her in a little slower now – nice and easy over the city. Yes, that's better. Straight ahead still.'

'But that would mean Quintay and Shara are hundreds of years old!' spluttered Tom in dismay.

The cheery pilot nodded. 'That would be right, according to earth measurements.'

'And the old couple are still having kids?' queried Malone. 'But *how*?'

'You mustn't judge everything by earth standards,' Micha told him. 'As I explained earlier, age is not a relevant factor here. And besides, childbirth here on Terran is different from on earth. There is no pain associated with bringing young ones into *this* world; in fact, quite the opposite – it is a very simple, effortless and pleasurable experience.'

Eve was astonished. 'That's the way I'd like to have *my* babies one day!' she said. And then another question drifted into her mind and puzzlement shaded her eyes. For a moment or two she didn't know whether she should even ask, but somehow it just slipped out.

'Micha, how is it that you seem to know so much about earth?'

'Yes,' added Tom, 'you talk as though you know all about our world, as though you've *been* there, even!'

The pilot grinned at them, his bright eyes laughing. 'What makes you think you've got a monopoly on space travel?'

'You mean you *have* been to earth!' gasped the freckle-faced boy.

But the only answer they received to that one was a cheeky wink and a sudden laugh.

'Look, there's the garden,' cried Eve. 'It's so lovely; so beautifully kept.'

'You must need a whole *army* of gardeners just to keep the weeds down,' remarked Malone.

Micha glanced at him. 'We have people who tend the garden, of course, but not in the way you're thinking.'

The officer laughed. He thought he knew when his leg was being pulled. 'C'mon . . . level with me. Who takes care of the weeds? And all that digging?'

'And the greenfly,' added Tom. '*Somebody* has to!'

'There you go again,' said the pilot. 'Comparing everything with earth. I told you, you can't view this world in the same light as your own.'

Malone stared at him, an uncertain smile hovering on his lips. 'Wait a minute . . . are you telling us that you don't get weeds in this garden?'

'Not so much as a root,' came the reply.

Malone wasn't convinced, but he thought he'd give him the benefit of the doubt. 'What's the secret – some wonder-compost? Something you spray on the soil, perhaps?'

Micha smiled. 'There's no secret, Captain. That's just the way The Maker planned it.'

'Then how come we got such a raw deal back home?' protested Malone. 'Why couldn't *we* have gardens without weeds?'

Micha hesitated before answering, then he turned to face the Captain, his bright eyes shining. 'It is not my place to say. But you will have an answer to all your questions before you leave here – that much I *can* say.'

'Oh, look at the deer!' called Becky – and suddenly all thoughts of weeds were gone.

'Yes, and the fawns,' said Eve. 'Aren't they sweet? We

79

didn't notice the animals before.'

'There are plenty of creatures to see, when you have the time,' Micha told them. 'Many species live in the garden, and of course there are many more outside, beyond the city.'

'I, er – I hope they're all friendly,' said Tom. 'Particularly if there are any round about the canyon.'

'Yes,' said Becky, 'especially as we have to return there on our own this afternoon.'

Micha grinned. 'You've nothing to fear from the wildlife on Terran, my friends – that's something else in which our two worlds differ.' He turned to Eve. 'Have you ever seen a fox lie down next to a rabbit?'

The girl giggled. 'Why, no, of course not.'

'Keep your eyes open, then. You may just – steady now, Zak! See the little reception committee down there? That's where we want to land.'

'Message received,' called the boy. 'Hold tight, everyone. Here we go!'

'And *don't* put us down in the lake!' chuckled Tom.

9

It was a great day for a picnic – bright and warm with a gentle breeze blowing in off the crystal waters of the lake and stirring the leaves of the overhanging trees. The food, too, was perfect – mouthwatering to look at and even better to eat! But this time all the dishes were Terran-style, delicious and surprising: a tantalizing mixture of exotic and subtle tastes, both savoury and sweet.

'More like a banquet than a picnic!' declared Tom, and once he'd tasted everything – yes, everything! – he informed his hosts that if ever he happened to be marooned in space he hoped it would be here on Terran. 'Yummy!' he exclaimed, and wished he hadn't, for he had to waste valuable eating time trying to explain the meaning of the word to the baffled Counsel members.

In fact there was plenty of talking at those tables by the water's edge. The air was soon buzzing with a rapid exchange of information and views. Zak was quite surprised; he had once thought that a first conversation with officials from another planet would be a very serious and high-flown affair, much like a first meeting of heads of state back on earth. But it was nothing like that. Everyone seemed more interested in the insignificant everyday things of the planets – and they even got round to the weather!

After the meal, relaxed and full, they left the tables and ambled down to a shady bank beside the lake where they settled in small groups on the soft, springy grass, laughing gently together and watching the graceful swanlike birds gliding to and fro on the sun-dappled waters.

It was wonderful. Even Zak and Becky found themselves

unwinding. To their surprise, they were able to lay aside their anxiety about their father and enjoy the happy peace. It was as though they were being allowed to forget about their quest and find relief from the pressures that had weighed so heavily upon them in the canyon.

But then something happened to disturb that peace for Zak. Glancing across to where Eve sat with one of the Counsel members, he saw something he didn't like. It was a smile. A smile that passed between Eve and her handsome young companion ... a smile that troubled him, and made him keep looking in their direction every few minutes from then on. He didn't know why, but he somehow felt uneasy for Eve. Yet that seemed absurd; she was having a good time; she wasn't in any danger.

But a while later, just as Quintay was getting to his feet, indicating that it was time for the meeting, Zak glimpsed that smile again, and this time a chill shot through him. Eve was clearly very taken with her new friend. But something about him now worried Zak deeply. The more he watched this stranger the more he was aware of a sense of foreboding.

This was ridiculous, he told himself. And as he stood up to leave with the others he tried desperately to push such thoughts from his mind. He couldn't. The foreboding persisted, and Zak moved closer to Eve as they walked through the garden. After a while he managed to steer her to one side, so that they were alone.

'Sath is a great guy,' Eve said, her eyes dancing.

'You certainly seemed to be having a good time,' said Zak.

'What's that supposed to mean?'

The boy hesitated. 'Listen, Eve, don't be offended – I know you were struck with that guy, but ... well, just take it easy, huh?'

The girl stopped and turned to face him. 'Zak Anderson, I do believe you're jealous!' – and she sounded quite pleased about it.

'No, I'm not. I'm worried about you, that's all. I – I've just got a bad feeling about the guy. I can't explain it, but . . .'

'Of course you can't explain it,' she interrupted, 'because it's irrational and you know it. Why, Sath is a wonderful person. He's charming and kind and funny – all the things I used to think you were!'

That hurt! And suddenly Zak knew just how he felt about Eve. He was jealous all right!

Eve made no effort to make him feel better. Turning to follow the others she said, 'Anyway, it's no good you asking me to stay away from him – he's offered to show me round the city after the meeting.'

Zak followed her, laying a hand on her shoulder. 'But you can't do that!'

She shrugged him off. 'And what's to stop me?'

'We've got a job to do!' he protested. 'We have to go back and look for Dad – you know that.'

She threw him an icy glance. 'You don't think I'm going back to that canyon, do you? I'm not going back to that spooky place for you or anybody. I'm sorry about your dad, but I'm sure you can find him without me.'

That hit a nerve too! 'You're being unreasonable, Eve. You *have* to come with us.'

'No, I don't.'

'You do!' he snapped. 'That – that's an order.'

She turned on him again, her eyes blazing. 'Well, I won't. What are you going to do about it – clap me in irons? Just leave me alone!' And she stormed away, hurrying to catch up with Sath.

Zak watched her go, seething with anger. He wasn't going to any stupid meeting, not with that Sath sitting there making eyes at Eve. And for the first time he wished he'd never set foot on the planet. There was something rotten about Sath, and for all he knew the others might be the same. Maybe it was all a big con, all this sweetness and light. Quintay and the others all seemed too good to be true, anyway. Perhaps it was all a cover – underneath they were probably as twisted as everyone else. The whole thing stank. If it hadn't been for his father, he would have rounded up his crew and blasted off there and then. And if Eve refused to go – well, that would be too bad. It would be *her* loss if she wanted to stay with her blue-eyed boyfriend.

'Everything all right, Zak?'

The voice took him by surprise, for he had been sure all the others were ahead of him.

'Micha!' he said, and turned away, confused. He didn't want the friendly pilot to see him like this. But it seemed he couldn't hide anything from those piercing eyes.

'He has a gift for upsetting people,' said Micha.

'Who, Sath?'

Micha nodded. 'That's why you're needed at the meeting, Zak.' And slowly the pieces began to fall into place.

'Oh, I see ... you mean, *he's* the one who's divided the Counsel over this cube business. What did you call him – a smooth talker? Well, you can say that again! If I get a chance I'll certainly tell the meeting what I think of him, you can count on that.'

Micha shook his head. 'That isn't what's needed, my friend. The time for words will come. First you must listen – with one ear tuned to Terran's future, and the other to your own past.'

'I don't understand,' said the boy.

'You will, when the time comes. Now we had better join the others.'

Zak glanced away. 'I don't know if I can – those two got me all fired up.'

Micha said nothing as he placed his hand on Zak's shoulder ... and moments later the boy felt his tension melting and that strange sense of peace flooding his mind.

He turned to face the pilot, shaking his head with incredulity. He felt fine. No anger towards Sath, no jealousy over Eve. Perfect calm. 'How do you do that?'

Micha smiled. 'It cannot be explained,' he said. 'It is the

peace that passes understanding. Have you not read of it? It's mentioned in The Book of The Lamb.'

'In the what?'

'The Book of The Lamb.' He smiled again. 'The key to all mysteries lies there ... including this one.'

Zak stood scratching his head, remembering. 'Wait a minute – Quintay mentioned something about a lamb; something to do with the garden.' He shot a glance at Micha. 'Say, d'you have a copy of that book?'

'Of course not,' said the pilot. 'But you do. That's the reason you're here.'

Zak stared at him, baffled. This whole thing was becoming more and more confusing. But before he had a chance to ask another question, Micha was tugging at his sleeve and hurrying away.

'Come on,' he called out. 'It wouldn't do to be late for the meeting.'

They entered the building – the small round building Tom had thought was a bandstand – and Zak was immediately struck by the sense of peace and quietness, an almost reverent hush. It was a welcoming place – pleasantly relaxing, airy and bright. It took a moment or two for him to identify the source of this brightness. At first he thought sunlight was streaming into the building; then he realized there were no windows.

'The cubes!' he breathed. 'The whole room is lighted by the cubes!'

The gently glowing cubes were the focal point of the whole room. Stacked within a towering, tiered framework they rose out of the centre of the floor, ringed by a circular desk. Around the desk the Counsel members and Zak's crew were seated in high-backed chairs, speaking in hushed tones as they waited for the meeting to begin.

Micha showed Zak to his seat then took his own place as Quintay leaned forward and moved his hand across a light-sensor built into the desk in front of him. Immediately the tower of cubes began moving slowly downwards into the floor until only the uppermost section, standing a metre high, was visible. It was then that the five earth visitors were reminded of the reason for this meeting. Set at the very top of the tower was a solitary cube that shone more brightly than all the others . . . the one cube that The Maker had instructed them not to touch.

Why? wondered the five. What mysterious knowledge did it contain? And why should such knowledge do the people of Terran more harm than good?

A moment later Quintay got to his feet and gazed soberly at the circle of faces, his steady eyes hushing every voice into silence. He glanced at Zak and the others and then he spoke: 'My friends, this is a truly historic day for Terran. It is a great honour and pleasure for us to welcome our visitors from planet earth, particularly as their visit was arranged by The Maker. As you will know by now, what brought them here was their quest to find Zak and Becky's father, and I'm pleased to say I was informed over lunch that they have found a vital clue that confirms Colonel Anderson's presence on this planet.'

The old man paused as a little ripple of excitement flowed around the circle, and then he went on: 'They would, of course, be continuing their search at this very moment except that The Maker requires their attendance at this meeting. The curious thing is, I have absolutely no idea why their presence here is so important – and come to that, nor do they – but no doubt the reason will unfold as the meeting progresses. First, however, I have asked that our friends say a few words, so I will hand over to them now.' He glanced at Zak, then sat down.

Zak leaned over and spoke quietly with Captain Malone, nodded, then rose to his feet. As commander of the mission this duty had fallen to him, and though he had quite forgotten about preparing a speech he launched into his salutations as though he had been practising all morning.

With confidence and humour Zak thanked Quintay for his welcome, remarked on the splendid lakeside lunch, then relayed greetings from earth, informing his hosts that they had brought with them on their journey an official plaque which they would complete and hand over to the Counsel in the hope that they would display it as a means of remembering this historic and auspicious occasion. This was met with nods and murmurs of approval, and he then went on to give a little background information to their mission. He finished in true statesmanlike fashion, expressing the hope that this initial contact between the two planets would pave the way for a lasting and mutually beneficial relationship – although there was one small snag. Unless they could rely on the space-warp – that mysterious intergalactic corridor which had plunged them into Terran's orbit – it seemed unlikely that other earth ships would ever be able to reach this distant planet.

'By our present rate of technological development,' he told them, 'it will be centuries before we can build spacecraft capable of flinging men to the other side of the universe.' He paused, glancing around the circle of faces. 'I guess that only underlines that we must be here for a very special purpose, and I for one can't wait to find out what that is.'

There was a murmur of agreement and Zak then handed back to Quintay. Then it was down to business.

There were one or two minor matters to discuss but these were quickly dealt with so that they could attend to the question of the cube. Quintay reminded the Counsel of the discussion so far, reiterating his staunch belief that the forbidden cube should remain untouched.

Sath was quick to rise to his feet, his arguments ready and finely polished.

'As I have said before, we only have *your* word that this cube *is* forbidden. With respect, Quintay, how can we be sure that your memory does not fail you? These instructions which you say you received from The Maker were given a long time ago.'

'My memory serves me well,' came the flat reply. 'I know what The Maker told me, and if you would ask him he will tell you the same.'

'Have *you* asked him of late?' Sath retorted dourly.

Quintay shook his head. 'I have no need. The Maker does not change his mind, you know that.'

'What I know,' Sath rejoined, 'is that we need the knowledge which that cube contains!' His burning eyes held Quintay's across the table. Then he sat down, turning to flash a smile at Eve. Zak saw it but, to his surprise, felt no desire to react. Malone, sitting next to him, leaned across to comment, but withdrew as one of the other Counsel members rose to his feet, his eyes on the lone cube gently glowing before him.

'Gentlemen, I see no reason why we cannot reach a settlement upon this issue. We have discussed this for many months and have now come to the position where we are equally divided in our opinion.'

'This is not a matter of opinion!' retorted Quintay. 'It is a matter of fact. I am disappointed in you, Garan. You know what The Maker has said.'

'I know what you have *told* me The Maker has said. When *I* ask The Maker he does not seem to give me a clearcut answer.'

'Perhaps you do not listen well enough,' came the swift reply. 'Or perhaps you do not really wish to know the truth. You seem set on availing yourself of the knowledge within that cube, regardless of The Maker's wishes.'

'If by that you mean I am for progress – yes, I believe in appropriating all the knowledge available to us.'

'But *this* knowledge is *not* available,' countered the old man. 'It is forbidden. The fact that it is sitting there under your nose does not alter that. Don't you see?'

'All I see,' said Garan, 'is that we are going round in circles. Why can't we agree to differ? To choose for ourselves? I say those who wish to hold the cube should hold it. Let it be a decision of the will.'

Quintay smiled across at the man, a tender, fatherly smile.

'My dear Garan, you know full well that is not the way we do things. In the past we have never acted on critical issues unless we have been unanimous. And even on the odd occasion when we have differed we have always adhered to the majority view.'

'But we do not have a majority.' This was a new voice – Garan's neighbour. 'We are equally divided, which we have never been before. Surely Garan is right: the proper course would be for each man to do what he believes to be right in his own eyes. That way each will be satisfied and we shall be done with our differences.'

Quintay eyed the man for a moment, then shook his head, wearily. 'I do not understand you, any of you. How can you be so blind, so stubborn?'

'*You* are the stubborn one, Quintay,' grated Sath, leaping to his feet. 'You refuse to allow your people to develop and progress as they might. Rich food awaits them and yet you let them feed on crumbs!'

Micha shot to his feet, his eyes blazing. 'That is a deception and you know it! The rich food of which you speak so lightly would most certainly turn out to be bitter poison! You know The Maker's words, Sath: "You shall not touch this cube, for in the day that you touch it you shall surely die!"'

'True!' shouted Quintay. 'Would you have us all die?'

'Come, come,' returned Sath, his eyes mellowing, his voice turning silky smooth. 'Must we entertain fables? You shall not die; the truth is that The Maker does not want you touching that cube because he knows that in the day that you touch it your eyes will be opened. You shall be as gods. Don't you see, The Maker is afraid for himself, not for you!' He thrust a stubborn finger towards the cube. 'Take that in your hand and you will know as he knows and see as he sees. Then you would have no need of him! That is the truth. Let your eyes be opened to it!'

'Hold your tongue!' roared Quintay. 'Do you not fear The Maker's wrath to speak of him so? I will have words with you in private, Sath. Now let this meeting be adjourned. We shall resume in the morning.'

He turned to Malone beside him, his face flushed.

'I apologise for this outburst, Captain.'

'No need,' said Malone. 'But if the meeting's over I think we should get back to the canyon and make use of the daylight hours. Roy's ship just has to be around there somewhere and ...'

'Excuse me,' Quintay interrupted, and brushed past him. Malone swung round to see him hurrying after Sath who was moving swiftly towards the door. Moments later the two men disappeared into the garden. He turned to Zak.

'Well, what d'you make of all that?'

'Beats me,' said the boy. 'Have you figured out why we were supposed to be here?'

'It's all a mystery to me,' said the Captain.

Zak nodded. 'Y'know, Micha said a strange thing to me before we came in here. He told me not to say anything in the meeting, but to listen, with one ear tuned to Terran's future and the other to our own past. Does that make any sense?'

It didn't – at least, not to Captain Malone. Then Tom and Becky came over and Zak asked them the same question. Tom merely looked blank, but Becky had been puzzling over some of the things she'd heard. She felt that Micha's comment was somehow a vital clue to the whole mystery.

'I don't have anything positive to go on,' said the girl, 'but I keep getting this strange feeling that a lot of things I'm hearing I've heard before. It happened on the way back with Micha this morning – d'you remember? He told me to think about it; that I might recall something important – and then again this afternoon, particularly when I was listening to Sath.'

'Hey, that fella gives me the creeps,' said Tom. 'I didn't care much for him. And why was Eve sitting next to him?

Has she gone off us?'

'I'm afraid that might be true,' said Zak sourly. 'At least, she's not talking to me at the moment. Didn't you see the way Sath was drooling over her down by the lake?'

'Aw, you're just jealous, Zak,' grinned Becky.

Her brother glanced at her. 'You're right, I am. But I don't feel mad about it like I did at first. It's that creepy Sath that worries me. I think he's got her under some sort of spell.'

Malone gave a short laugh. 'You're right, you *are* jealous!' He glanced round. 'Anyway, where *is* Eve? We'd better be making a move.'

'She's already gone,' said Zak. 'Didn't you see her? She left just after Quintay.'

'I'll go and get her,' said Becky, turning towards the door.

But Zak called out, 'She won't come. She's already told me she's going with Sath this afternoon. He's going to show her round the city or something.'

'She can't do that. We need her.' And with that Becky ran out into the sunlit garden.

'Come on,' said Zak, 'let's get moving. Has anyone seen Micha?'

They found the pilot down by the lake, checking over the spherical ship before the flight to the canyon.

'All set?' he asked with a cheery grin.

'I guess so,' answered Zak. 'We're just waiting for Becky; she's trying to persuade Eve to come with us – not that she'll succeed.' He glanced back towards the round building. 'I don't like leaving her here, not with him.'

Micha nodded. 'She'll be all right. But what about you? Happy about flying this thing on your own?'

'We'll be fine.'

'Look,' said Tom, 'here comes Becky now – but no sign of Eve.'

Zak grunted. 'I told you so.'

The girl came running up, panting. 'For a minute I thought you'd gone without *me* too!' she gasped.

'She's not coming, then?' said Malone.

Becky shook her head. 'He's going to take her round the city, then she's going to show him over the space-cruiser.'

'The nerve!' rasped Zak. 'She can't do that!'

'Forget it,' said Malone. 'It won't do any harm. Now come on, or we'll never get there.'

Zak turned to Micha. 'Any ideas? I mean, where we should search?'

'Follow the voice within,' said the pilot, and then he turned to face Tom, smiling gently. 'Don't simply rely on logic.'

Tom flushed a little as those bright eyes bored into him once more, but this time the boy felt no compulsion to turn away. Micha's look was somehow reassuring. He even wished the pilot could come with them. And as if in response to that thought Micha said, 'You don't need me this time; I'm sure you'll be all right. But if you stay after dark you'll find a couple of flashlights behind the rear seats.'

'Oh, but what about flying home in the dark?' said Becky.

'That's all right,' Zak told her. 'We simply put the ship on automatic – right, Micha?'

He nodded. 'Just programme your destination. The ship will do the rest.' And then he gestured for them to climb aboard.

They stepped inside and got themselves seated, then Zak turned to Micha, saluting genially.

'Follow the voice within,' muttered the boy as he took the silver rod in his hand. Then they heard the engines whirr into life somewhere behind them, and moments later they were moving, zooming up into the great blue sky.

They touched down in the canyon beneath a late afternoon sun already throwing shadows along the towering rocky walls. There were two, maybe three, hours of daylight left. As Becky stepped out on to the stony ground of the canyon she remembered that darkness had fallen quickly the previous night and she was glad of the flashlights.

'Should we take them with us?' she asked Zak.

'Not yet,' replied the boy. 'Let's have another look at the place where the fin was buried, then we can decide where to search.'

They clambered over the boulders and picked their way through the scattered rocks until they reached the place, and stood there looking around, wondering what they should do next. Wondering . . . and listening. It was Zak's idea, and he was in command.

But eventually Tom could bear the silence no longer. 'Come on, let's do something,' he groaned. 'I feel stupid standing around here like this.'

'Sh!' said Zak, listening hard – then he gave up and glared reproachfully at him. 'I nearly had something then.'

'What, the inner voice?' chuckled Tom, who found the whole idea rather humorous.

'Don't knock it,' snapped Zak. 'It may be our only chance of finding Dad. You know what Micha said.'

'I know, I know,' retorted Tom. 'But surely we ought to be *doing* something. Can't we start searching?'

'And where do you suggest we begin?' countered Zak, gesturing widely across the canyon.

'I don't know,' he muttered, 'but I'm not sure that I can

believe in this inner voice stuff.'

Zak rolled his eyes in despair and turned away, but Malone moved in and laid a hand on Tom's shoulder.

'I know what you mean, Tom, but you have to realize we're dealing with things here that were previously outside our experience. I mean, two days ago you wouldn't have believed in any number of things we've seen here on Terran – like driving through a solid wall, for instance.'

'Or flying a spacecraft by thought-waves,' said Zak.

'Or people who never die and a garden without weeds,' added Becky.

Tom looked at each of them in turn, then nodded, thrusting his hands into his pockets. 'I guess not. But how come *I* don't hear anything?'

'Because you're not listening hard enough,' said Becky, squeezing his arm. Then she said, 'Tom, do you believe in The Maker?'

The boy glanced at her, then looked down, pushing the dust about with the toe of his boot. That was a big question. At last he said, 'I suppose so. I mean, I *think* so.'

'There's your problem,' smiled the girl. 'You can hardly expect to hear the voice of someone if you're not even sure they exist. I wasn't sure either, but Zak's right – this may be our only chance of finding Dad. So I decided to give it a try. I listened – and I heard.'

Zak whirled round. 'You *did*?'

She looked diffident. 'Well, I think so – but I'm not going to say what until someone else confirms it.'

'All right,' said Zak, 'let's try it again.'

They fell silent and before long Zak found himself turning away from the canyon to face the dense, dark undergrowth of the valley.

'I – I think we have to go this way.'

Becky came and stood beside him. 'That's what I got,' she grinned.

'Hey, I think you're right,' chuckled Tom, and immediately

94

started marching off towards the sprawling greenery. 'Come on, everyone.'

Zak and Becky turned to Malone in enquiry, but the Captain just shrugged. 'I think I'm going deaf,' he laughed. 'I'll just follow the majority.' And with a sweep of his hand he said, 'After you!'

'Flashlights!' cried Becky, suddenly remembering, and she took off towards the ship. 'Wait for me, won't you?'

It wasn't so much a valley, they decided – more a part of the canyon where the vegetation had taken over. Various species of pine tree dominated the place, their great solid shapes towering over a jungle of waist-high grasses and enormous, billowing bushes, many with exotic blooms and heady fragrances. There were no paths, of course, so it was hard work beating a way through the foliage.

'Bit of a mixture,' remarked Zak. 'One minute a botanist's dream, the next a gardener's nightmare!'

'Yes,' agreed Tom. 'It's a bit like fighting your way through the hot-house at Kew Gardens!'

'The *what*?'

'Kew Gardens,' he repeated. 'It's a famous botanical garden in London. I used to live near there.' He stopped and looked around him, puffing and perspiring. 'Does anyone know where we're going?'

'Not much further,' called Zak.

'Oh!' marvelled Tom. 'I'm glad you're still in radio contact!'

Shortly they came to a sort of clearing where Zak stopped and looked about him.

'Well, where to now?' enquired Malone.

Zak glanced at him. 'I'm not sure, sir.'

Tom scowled. 'What, you mean you've run out of signals?'

Zak stared at him. 'Either that, or we've arrived at where we need to be.'

Tom blinked. 'Huh?'

'Let's take a look around,' said Zak. 'Look for any clue –

anything that might be the next pointer. Come on, spread out and search. I'm sure we haven't gone wrong – I know we're on the right track.'

Two or three minutes later they heard Becky calling out, 'Zak! Zak, look here! I think I've found something!'

The others glanced around. They could hear her, but she was nowhere to be seen.

'Where are you, Becky?'

'Up here!'

'There she is!' gasped Tom, returning to the clearing. 'Hey, what's she doing up there?'

They followed Tom's finger and saw the girl perched on a rock some way up the side of the canyon.

'Becky!' cried Zak. 'Are you all right? How did you get up there?'

'I'm fine,' she replied. 'There are rocks you can climb up, like steps. There's a sort of cave here – at least, an opening in the rock, like a tunnel.'

'Wait there!' shouted her brother.

There was a small ledge at the mouth of the cave and within a couple of minutes all four of them were perched there, peering into the darkness. The tunnel seemed to run deep into the rock wall of the canyon – so deep that not even the powerful beams of the flashlights could reach the end.

'Where do you suppose it leads?' asked Becky, still staring into the deep darkness.

'I guess there's only one way to find out,' said Zak. He glanced at Malone. 'D'you think it's safe?'

The Captain shrugged his shoulders. 'Only one way to find *that* out, too.'

They had to crawl on their hands and knees to get through the first part of the tunnel, but it was wide enough for them to go in pairs. Zak and Malone went first with the flashlights, Tom and Becky following close behind. The stone floor was beautifully smooth – worn away by an underground stream at some time in the past, they thought – but the rock was cold and damp. They were glad when the tunnel opened out into a much wider cavern and they were able to stand up.

Here the tunnel began to run downwards and soon they could no longer see the little patch of light that marked the entrance. It was growing colder too, and Becky found herself shivering against the dampness. But the worst bit, she thought, was the way the jutting rocks threw ghostly shadows above them from the powerful beams of the flashlights.

'Like spooky, staring faces,' she thought as the occasional studs of glittering ore shone down at her like bright, staring eyes. At any moment she expected one of these dreadful faces to come to life and fill the cavern with an evil, haunting laugh. Then she told herself she was being silly, but that didn't seem to help.

'What a horrible place!' she called to Zak, and jumped as an eerie echo answered her back, '. . . horrible place! . . . horrible place!'

Zak glanced over his shoulder, scowling. 'Sh! Don't call out like that!' His voice was a low murmur. 'We don't want to make any more noise than necessary.'

'Why?' whispered his sister, her eyes round with alarm.

'Because,' said Zak, stopping and turning to her, 'vibrations can cause a landslide. You go shouting your head off in here and we could have the whole lot caving in on us.'

'Oh, that's nice!' quipped Tom. 'Now he tells us!'

'I'm not saying it's inevitable,' Zak answered him, 'but we just don't know what condition the roof of this place is in.' And he flashed his torch around at the rough, rocky ceiling.

'Zak, I don't like it,' Becky whispered, and she clutched hold of his arm. 'It's spooky in here!'

He shook her off, irritated. 'Don't go getting squeamish,' he complained, 'or I'll start wishing we hadn't brought you.'

'What's going on back there?' Malone called in a low voice. He had gone on a little way when Zak had turned back for Becky.

'Nothing,' Zak replied in a loud whisper. 'We're just

coming.' He turned to Becky. 'Come on, Sis, where's that indomitable Anderson spirit? Just keep close to me and think about Dad. For all we know he might be round the next corner.'

They went on, moving quickly yet cautiously as the tunnel began to twist and turn, bending first this way and then that. In some places it was wide enough for them to walk four abreast and in others so narrow that they had to ease forward in single file. All the time it was heading downwards.

'We must be about level with the canyon floor by now,' ventured Captain Malone. He glanced at Zak, pacing along beside him. 'I'd say we must have walked almost a mile already. You sure you want to go on?'

'I'm sure,' Zak told him. 'I know it sounds crazy, but I've got such a strong feeling that we're on the right track and . . .' His words faded and suddenly he stopped still. Malone halted a step or two later.

'What is it, Zak?'

'Do you feel that?' said the boy. 'Do you feel the air? There's a draught blowing down this passage – and a draught means an opening of some sort.'

Malone shook his head. 'I don't feel anything.'

'Turn off the flashlights. Maybe we'll see daylight ahead,' said Zak, quite forgetting that by now it would be almost dark outside. He also failed to notice that Tom and Becky were lagging a few paces behind and that they hadn't heard him say anything about dowsing the lights. Thrust into sudden darkness, Becky panicked. When Tom reached out to comfort her she was sure she was about to be strangled by some terrible creature and let out the most terrifying scream that echoed back and forth through that dark place, bouncing off one wall after another until it died away in the distance.

'Jupiter!' cried Zak as he and Malone activated the flashlights again and swung the beams round at Becky. 'What in space d'you think you're . . .'

He didn't finish because at that moment their breath was caught by a rumbling sound – a distant, threatening roar.

They glanced at one another, not daring to move, their hearts suddenly racing. Anxiously they waited, ears straining for that awful sound again . . . but it didn't come. It was a full minute before Zak found his voice, but this time he was careful to speak in whispers.

'You idiot! What did you go and do that for?'

'Well, how did I know you were going to turn out the lights?'

Zak ignored that. 'I told you, you'll have the place caving in on us. That rumble was only a warning! Now come on, and for Pete's sake keep your voices down.'

Without another word they moved on, chilled with fear, and each of them, even Zak, wishing they had not come. Maybe it had been a mistake to enter this miserable place with its damp walls and clammy air. It was so cold now that each of them was shivering freely. Perhaps they should turn back and return tomorrow with the proper clothing and equipment; maybe they could find a guide too – someone who knew the canyon and its caves.

It all made so much sense and Zak was on the verge of giving the order to quit when suddenly his spirits leapt as he felt a draught upon his face again, this time much stronger. Excited, he glanced at Malone.

'Feel it now – the draught?'

The Captain nodded. 'It can't be far to the opening.'

And within a minute they knew they were there. The tunnel narrowed again around the last bend until they had to crawl on hands and knees. The cool draught blew strongly here and just a few metres farther on there appeared to be a small opening.

This time Zak and Becky went first, hearts in their mouths. Could their Dad really be on the other side?

And as they neared the opening – a tiny opening barely wide enough for even one to squeeze through – they heard the most astonishing thing.

'Music!' breathed Becky.

'Mozart!' gasped Zak.

'Dad's favourite!' they chorused.

99

11

There was no mistaking it – the sweet strains of classica[l]
music flowing from somewhere beyond that opening wa[s]
Mozart. And that just had to mean they'd found their father –
or was this another of Terran's wonders?

Eagerly they crawled forward until Zak was able to shin[e]
the flashlight into the hole . . . only to see a large rock block[-]
ing their view, just an arm's length beyond the opening.

'Think we can shift it?' asked Becky, as the stream of air
fluffed her hair.

Zak handed his sister the flashlight and reached into the
hole with both arms to push away the obstruction. Grunting
and puffing, he pushed away for a while, but quickly gave up.

'It's no good,' he said. 'I can't get the leverage. I managed
to rock it slightly, but I can't get the pressure with my arms.'

As he spoke he twisted himself round so that his feet went
through the hole and his back was up against the side of the
tunnel.

'This might do it . . .' He pushed his hardest with both feet
squarely on the rock. 'Yes . . . yes, its going!'

The grating noise of rock on rock confirmed this – and
moments later, with a mighty push, the boy's legs thrust out
straight. 'Done it!'

Then they heard a loud clattering as the rock crashed and
bounced down into some sort of abyss, finally rolling to a halt
some way below.

They exchanged anxious smiles. 'Good job the rock was
there,' said Zak. 'That could have been one of *us* taking a
dive!'

But the next thing surprised them even more – the music

suddenly stopped! Puzzled, Becky handed Zak the flashlight and he shone it into the hole, wriggling through up to his waist. Moments later his voice came back to her, electric with excitement. '*Excalibur*! We've found it! It's here!'

Becky turned to Tom and Malone, squatting behind her. With bright, dancing eyes she exclaimed, 'We've found her! We've found *Excalibur*! Dad just has to be here!' And in that awkward, cramped space she somehow managed to give the others a great big hug.

Very soon they had all passed through that tiny opening and found themselves perched precariously on a narrow ledge. But while they gazed down on the lost probe ship with a bubbly mixture of relief and joy they felt a chilling sense of mystery. From their rocky perch some thirty metres from the ground they shone their flashlights all around to discover that the tunnel had brought them out part way up a huge natural shaft – a vast, deep hole not much wider than *Excalibur* itself. Though it was pitch dark they could tell they were in a shaft rather than a cavern because of the powerful flow of air. But how ever did the Starforce ship get down here? It certainly hadn't landed there, and though the ship had clearly taken a battering at some time or other it didn't look as if it had crashed into the hole. Ridiculous as it seemed, the only explanation could be that *Excalibur* had simply been lowered into the shaft and placed at the bottom.

'And look!' gasped Tom, training Malone's flashlight on the ship again. 'Someone's piled rocks on top of the personnel hatch! Why ever would they do that?'

Malone glanced at him. 'Well, it certainly wasn't to keep people from getting in.'

'Oh no!' cried Becky, suddenly fearful for her father's safety – and she yelled out, 'Dad! *Dad*!'

Captain Malone clapped a silencing hand to her mouth and she looked up at him in alarm.

'Don't call out,' he told her softly. 'We don't know if there's anyone else around.'

101

The girl moved his hand away and with trembling lip said, 'What do you mean? Who else *could* be around?' But it didn't take much figuring out and moments later she exclaimed, 'Then Eve was right! We *do* have an enemy on this planet!'

The Captain glanced at Zak, then back at the girl. 'It looks that way, Becky.' In the glare of the flashlights he looked down again at the rocks piled over the ship's hatchway. 'And at a guess I'd say whoever buried that fin in the canyon also stacked those stones on your father's only exit. We weren't meant to find that fin, just as we were never meant to find *Excalibur*.'

'Then someone's been keeping Dad a prisoner!' said Zak angrily. 'But who? Why?'

'Maybe your dad will know the answer to that! Come on, let's find a way down.'

Getting down to the floor of the shaft was not as difficult as they had expected. There were plenty of foot- and hand-holds in the rocky wall and by climbing down in pairs, each pair sharing a flashlight, they were all down within minutes.

Together they went to the silent ship, each of them trembling slightly with an uneasy mixture of anticipation and fear as they worked to clear the hatchway of rocks. Becky almost gave up half-way through, suddenly feeling sick at the thought that all this would turn out to be a waste of time; that when at last they had gained entrance to *Excalibur* they would find her father dead. But then Zak reminded her about the music. Oh, how their father loved his Mozart! And by the time the last rock had been shifted – a huge, flat stone covering the entire hatchway – she was eager to enter the lost ship.

Malone jerked the sliding door open and peered inside. Darkness. He motioned to Zak who stepped forward and climbed down into the ship, Becky following. Once inside they stopped, shining the flashlight around. It felt pleasantly warm and there was the vague smell of hot food, but somehow Zak couldn't bring himself to go forward.

'Dad?' he called out. 'Dad, are you there? This is Zak.'

'And Becky, Dad. We're both here. Captain Malone, too.'

But no answer came. There was complete silence.

Zak took a step forward. 'Dad, we heard your music. Are you there? Are you OK?'

Again there was no reply, but suddenly some lights flickered on overhead, bathing them in a bright glow. The rest of the ship remained in darkness. Zak glanced at his sister, smiling faintly.

'He's here, Sis.'

But before Becky could respond another voice broke the silence.

'Oh my gosh!'

Together they swung round, catching him in the beam of the flashlight – a tall, well-built figure in Starforce uniform, with a weighty wrench in his hand poised as a weapon.

'Dad!'

As he stepped forward they rushed to him. He dropped the wrench and cried out, 'Kids!'

He hugged them, an arm round each of them, crying a little as again he blurted out, 'Oh my gosh! Zak! Becky! Thank goodness it's you! I – I thought it was a trick!'

There was a good deal more hugging and then Captain Malone appeared, grinning.

'Jack!' roared the Colonel and he came forward to greet his friend. 'Boy, was I ever glad to see you!'

'You ol' son-of-a-gun!' beamed Malone. 'I knew we'd turn you up sooner or later! Hey, you're looking good!'

Roy Anderson opened his mouth to reply but Tom had chosen that moment to make a spectacular entrance, missing his footing on the way in and landing spread-eagled on the floor.

He got up, making a little joke about learning to fly, and was introduced, flushing slightly when the famous astronaut gave him an unexpected hug.

'I'm glad to see you, son – real glad!'

They talked a moment longer, then the Colonel showed them through to *Excalibur*'s living quarters. They settled in the relaxation bay.

'You're looking good, Roy,' the Captain said again.

His buddy nodded. 'Well, I've been trying to keep myself fit. Little else to do all this time.'

'And what about the beard? You know, I think it suits you.'

Roy Anderson stroked his chin. 'Oh, this is my protest. I swore I wouldn't shave it off till I got out of this mess.' He grinned and glanced happily at Zak and Becky seated either side of him. 'And it's coming off first chance I get,' he added.

There was more small talk as the initial excitement passed, and then the questions began to flow.

What were they doing here? How did they find him? And where were they, anyway? The prisoner had no idea about what had been happening outside.

Zak eagerly explained their mission, with Becky filling in the details and the others chipping in with their own comments from time to time. Tom was particularly keen to tell how they had stumbled upon the broken fin in the canyon and Zak smiled to himself, remembering that at the time Tom didn't even believe that *Excalibur* had landed there.

The whole strange story amazed Colonel Anderson, but nothing surprised him more than to learn that they had made the journey in his own space-cruiser.

'With new engines, of course,' added Zak. 'They gave us the same power unit as you've got here.' He glanced towards the flight deck. 'What sort of shape is she in, Dad? You took quite a battering when you force-landed in the canyon.'

The Colonel nodded. 'I know. I haven't been outside, of course, but I can tell there's quite a bit of structural damage. The systems are functioning normally, though. I've been running the engines every day to keep the power cells boosted.' And with a rueful smile he added, 'Not that I was going anywhere.'

'That's what beats me,' remarked Malone. 'How you got stuck down this darn hole.'

His old friend shook his head. 'The whole thing is a mystery to me, Jack, from the moment I lost control to being dumped down here.'

'That's how it happened, huh? Engines malfunctioned.'

'I'm not even sure about that,' replied the Colonel. 'I remember being sucked into the space-warp and I recall coming round to find that I was in orbit of this planet. The computer-log shows that all systems were normal at that point, but suddenly it was as though the ship was being taken over – like it was being guided, but not by me.' He gave a short laugh. 'I know it sounds crazy, but it seemed as if some giant hand just grabbed hold of the ship and hurled it down to the planet, right into the canyon. I thought it was curtains when I realized there were rocks and boulders everywhere. How the ship stayed in one piece I'll never know.' He turned to Zak. 'Say, did you ever find the source of those distress signals?'

The boy shook his head. 'Never did.'

'Hm,' said the Colonel. 'That's really weird.'

Becky reached across and took hold of her father's hand, smiling up at him. 'Were you hurt when the ship crashed, Dad?'

He returned her smile. 'Got a bump on the head, honey, and passed out for a couple of hours. I think the movement of the ship brought me round. It was the strangest thing, as if that hand grabbed hold of us again. Lifted the ship up and set it right down in this pit.'

Malone said, 'You didn't see any other craft? Something with lifting gear? They've got some pretty fancy technology on this planet.'

'No other machines,' the Colonel said flatly. 'And I can tell you, by that time I was getting a little jumpy. But that was nothing to what I had coming. After I'd been dumped down here I waited for about an hour before venturing outside. The sensors didn't indicate any sort of alien activity so I grabbed a hand-laser and opened up the hatch – and there was this character standing there staring down at me.'

Tom gave an enormous gulp. 'W-what sort of character?'

'Well, he was humanoid – almost normal-looking, I'd say – except for the eyes. Boy, there was fire in those eyes! Literally, I mean – they glowed bright red! It was pretty clear that he meant trouble, so I decided it would have to be "shoot first, questions later".'

'*And*?' gasped Zak.

His father grimaced. 'Before I'd even raised the laser that guy shot out his hand and something like a thunderbolt knocked me off the steps and left me in a heap on the floor. I mean that was some power he was carrying.'

'You didn't see any sort of weapon?' asked Malone.

The Colonel laughed shortly. 'Jack, that character didn't need a weapon – he *was* a weapon!'

'What happened next?' spluttered Tom.

'It was extraordinary. He came down into the ship and I leapt up to have another go, with my fists this time, but when I took a swing at him I couldn't get through – my knuckles stopped dead on some sort of force-field.' He showed them his right hand. 'See that burn mark? I tell you, that guy was walking electricity.'

'So what did you do?' gasped Becky.

Her father shrugged. 'What else could I do – I asked him what he wanted!'

He smiled, and they all laughed.

'And you know what he was after?' He glanced at Malone. 'You'll never believe this, Jack – the guy wanted the Bible!'

'The *what*?'

'He wanted the micro-tapes of the Bible from the video-library. That's all he wanted.'

'And you handed them over?'

'You bet I did!' He pointed to the ship's entertainments unit, a similar piece of equipment to that which had been in constant use aboard the space-cruiser. 'I found those tapes in a flash and that guy snatched them away and crushed them in his hand like so much paper.' He shook his head, wondering. 'Then when he opened his fist . . . all that was left was a little pile of ash, still smouldering.' He glanced at the others, one at a time. 'Can you believe that? I mean it was weird, like a bad dream.'

Captain Malone nodded, his face grave. 'And did he leave after that?'

'After telling me I was lucky to still be alive. He said he wasn't going to kill me yet, in case he had further use for me. Then he just turned round and walked out. Next thing I heard those stones being piled over the hatch.'

'Oh, Daddy, how horrible!' cried Becky, and she flung herself upon him, her arms round his neck. 'Thank goodness you're safe!'

Malone said, 'Well, that guy must have had some strength, Roy. I tell you, it was hard enough removing those stones; I'd sure hate to try lifting them up there.'

Zak nodded. 'He must have had help.'

'I don't think so,' said his father. 'I doubt if he'd have needed it, anyway. That guy was super-charged.'

By now Tom could hardly believe his ears. He'd never heard such a story! 'And he's not been back, sir?' he asked.

'Not in all this time. But I thought he was on his way when I heard the disturbance outside earlier.'

'Was that when you heard a rock crashing down?' asked Zak. 'And when you turned off the music?'

The Colonel nodded. 'I'd prepared a little surprise for him so I quickly got ready.'

'Oh, so that's why you had the wrench in your hand!' smiled Becky, sitting up.

'Well, that was my back-up plan,' grinned her father. 'I figured that a little shock treatment might be more effective, so I wired up the floor section beneath the hatchway. Once he'd set foot on it I was going to run a few thousand volts through him. I was hiding back there with the switch-gear, all ready to turn him into a crisp.'

'Wow! Then we're lucky to be alive!' gasped Zak.

'Yes, you might have turned *us* into crisps!' said Becky, in alarm.

Their father smiled fondly at them, but said nothing.

Tom said, 'Colonel Anderson, do you think you'd recognize this – this enemy, if you saw him again?'

'I'm not likely to forget him,' came the flat reply. 'Why, does it sound like some character you've met?'

'No, sir, it does not – thank goodness! But . . .'

'But why should he want the Bible?' Zak cut in. 'I mean, just to destroy it like that?'

'Look, why don't we save the questions,' suggested Malone. 'We ought to be getting back. Besides, I don't think it's wise to hang around here longer than necessary – just in case our friend does return. Are you ready to travel, Roy?'

'Just let me grab a couple of things and I'll be with you,' said the astronaut. He lifted Becky aside and got to his feet. 'I tell you, Jack, I'll be glad to see the back of *Excalibur* for a while.'

They wasted no time in preparing to return through the tunnel. Colonel Anderson kitted everyone out with additional clothing, handed out a couple of extra flashlights, clipped his hand-laser to his belt, grabbed his things and they were off.

Zak reminded them to talk as little as possible in the tunnel, and then only in whispers – but keeping quiet was a tall order! With the discovery of what had happened to Colonel Anderson there were now so many more questions that demanded answers.

What strange and mighty power had caused *Excalibur* to crash and then lifted it into the pit?

Who was the mysterious and powerful man who had overpowered Colonel Anderson and then imprisoned him in his own spacecraft?

Why should this enemy go to so much trouble merely to get his hands on the micro-tapes of the Bible, and then only to destroy them? That certainly didn't make sense. To them the Bible didn't have much to do with the scientific world of the twenty-first century. Its inclusion in any library – including Starforce video-libraries – was purely on the grounds of cultural and historical interest.

But this threw up another, even more gaping question: why should a book that seemed to matter little on its own planet be important on another?

'It doesn't make sense,' Becky told Zak as they strode up through the dank and chilly cave. 'The Bible's just a book of stories; hardly anybody reads it now.'

'Yes, but it *used* to be important,' said Zak, who wanted to test a theory.

'So what? A hundred years ago 40 per cent of Americans went to church. They're turning the places into warehouses now. We've grown up.'

'But suppose we're wrong, and earlier generations were right?'

The girl glanced at him in the glow of the flashlights. 'What are you getting at?'

'Suppose we've goofed – that the Bible is actually far more important than we realized, and that in some way our two planets are linked by it?'

'Linked by the Bible? But how?'

'I don't know. But someone here on Terran does. Someone, somewhere knows enough about the Bible to think that it poses a threat ... a threat so serious that they had to destroy those tapes at all cost.'

'Oh, Zak, that's too ridiculous for words! There has to be a better explanation than that.'

'Hang on,' said her brother, 'we're coming to the place where we heard that rumbling noise.' He motioned to everyone to keep quiet and they passed through in silence. Then the tunnel opened out and there was room for Tom to join them, walking three abreast, with Malone and Colonel Anderson bringing up the rear.

They told Tom their thoughts so far, and he said, 'But how could anyone on Terran know anything about an old book out of our past?'

Tom's words rang a bell. 'Hold on,' said Zak. 'Micha said something about the past! Now what was it? It was before the meeting, in the garden ...'

'I remember,' said Becky. 'You told us after the meeting. He said you were to listen with one ear to the future and the other to the past.'

'That's it,' said her brother. 'Almost, anyway. He said, listen with one ear to *Terran's* future and with the other to *our* past. He could have meant the Bible – like you said, Tom: a book out of our *past*!'

Now Becky's mind was racing. 'Yes, I – I think you could be right, Zak. And d'you remember how I said that certain things sounded familiar to me, as though I'd heard them before?'

He nodded. 'There was something Micha said when we were flying back to the city this afternoon, wasn't there?'

'And in the meeting, too!' she said, her heart now pounding with the anticipation of discovery. 'There were lots of things – oh, if only I could remember what they were! I'm sure they have something to do with this.'

'Well, let's back up a bit. What were we talking about on that journey?'

'About how Quintay was always having driving accidents,' chuckled Tom.

The girl glared at him. 'It was nothing like that. It was something serious.'

'I'm sure poor old Quintay thought crashing his egg-thingy was *very* serious at the time!' retorted the boy.

'Oh, you know what I mean,' hissed Becky.

'The cubes!' said Zak, a little too loudly. And then he whispered, 'Remember? – about the cube they mustn't touch.'

His sister nodded thoughtfully. 'That's right. That was one of the things. And then, when I was listening to Sath in the meeting, it was like – like listening to echoes of a distant voice, as if I'd heard it all before. But I can't for the life of me think where or when!' She grunted impatiently. 'It's so infuriating!'

Zak thought about it for a moment. 'Look, Quintay said that the reason for our being here had something to do with that meeting. And some of the things that were said at the meeting you think you've heard before, Becky.' He paused, fitting the pieces together in his mind. 'Could it be, then – and I know this sounds kinda crazy – could it be that what you heard is something you've read in the Bible? Long ago, almost forgotten.'

Tom and Becky stared at him.

'Zak, that is one heck of a wild idea!' groaned the boy.

'No, it's not,' countered Becky. 'I mean, I know it *sounds* fantastic – a garden without weeds, people who never die, and all that stuff. But it sounds faintly familiar too. But as for it coming out of the Bible . . . I just can't be sure. I can't even remember *reading* the Bible.'

'Well, maybe you had it read *to* you,' suggested Zak – and the words were like a great light flashing on! Instantly they stopped and stood staring at each other, wide-eyed.

'Dad!' they chorused.

And it was Dad who nearly tripped over them, stopping so suddenly in that narrow tunnel!

'Hey, no signals!' chided the Colonel. 'What is this – you guys doing a spot check on my reflexes?'

'Sorry, Dad,' said Zak. 'It's just that we think we may have hit on some sort of key to the mystery of why we're here . . .'

'And now we've got stuck,' added Becky. 'We need your help.'

'OK. What's the problem?'

Zak glanced at Becky and nodded.

She said, 'When I was small, when you and Mom used to read to me, did you ever tell me stories from the Bible?'

Her father looked down at her in the glow of the flashlights, smiling his curiosity. 'Well, I guess so. Your grandma did, of course – Grandma Anderson. She was a great one for Bible stories. But that was before we moved down to Texas. You were both pretty young then, so maybe you don't remember. What's this about, anyway?'

Well, where should they begin? There seemed so much to tell and they agreed to tell it as they walked on. Up out of the dismal tunnel they went, then down through the clinging undergrowth and shadowy trees, each of them telling what they knew.

Together they told the Colonel about The Maker and the garden and the amazing cubes . . . about Quintay and Shara

112

and the city that shone like gold ... about Micha and Sath and the People's Counsel ... and the argument over the forbidden cube.

They told about their own thoughts, too: about the enemy and the Bible and things half remembered ... about voices from the past.

Was there a connection here somewhere?

'It was just like I'd heard those things before, Dad,' Becky finished.

Her father glanced at her. 'You mean like you were hearing the story of Adam and Eve all over again, is that it?'

The girl stopped and caught hold of her father's arm. The others, too, turned to face the Colonel, their curiosity aroused.

'What d'you mean?' asked Becky.

The bearded face laughed. 'Well, it seems I remember my Bible stories better than you, young lady. The garden of Eden, Adam and Eve, the forbidden fruit – doesn't that ring any bells?'

'Why, yes,' said the girl with surprise. 'Yes, it does!'

Zak was scratching his head, stirring the memories and fitting the pieces together. 'Dad, d'you mean that what's happening here on Terran is Eden all over again?'

'It's pretty close, from what you've told me. Even the name of the planet's close to our own.'

'Terran?' said Malone, who was intrigued with his friend's theory.

'Sure. Terra, Terran. Terra means earth, remember?'

Tom laughed. 'But, Colonel, surely that's just a myth, that Adam and Eve stuff! There has to be a more rational explanation.'

'Maybe there is,' shrugged the astronaut. 'But it seems to me you're pretty short on options at the moment. Shall we keep moving?'

They pressed on, trudging through the waist-high grass and ducking under the sprawling creepers until at last they were back in the rocky canyon. There they pointed out the place where they had dug up the fin, and Colonel Anderson described again how *Excalibur* had crash-landed among the boulders, but those things now seemed less important than the tangled mystery before them. It certainly seemed difficult to accept that the solution might lie in such an unlikely theory, but the more they talked the more parallels there seemed to be.

'You can call them coincidences, if you like,' said the Colonel, 'but for my money there are just too many of them.'

'Say, would you recap on that Eden stuff for me, Roy,' said Captain Malone. His knowledge of the Bible was somewhat thin, and he was having trouble following the connections.

'Sure – though I'm a little rusty on all this myself. As I recall, God put Adam and Eve in a beautiful garden that needed little tending – just like your garden here in the city – and told them they could eat whatever they fancied, except the fruit of a certain tree. That was out of bounds. It seemed that this worked OK until along came the serpent and tempted them.' He laughed shortly. 'I guess they just couldn't resist the curiosity any longer, 'cos they ate the fruit – and we've been picking up the pieces ever since!'

'How come?' said Malone.

'It's what they used to call the "fall". Didn't you ever hear that?'

Malone glanced at him. 'You mean earth was once a perfect world, but Adam lost it for the entire human race?' He shook his head. 'Gee, that was a dumb thing to do.'

The Colonel laughed. 'It wasn't too neighbourly of him, was it!'

Zak turned to him. 'What were you saying about the fruit, Dad? I mean, what was so special about it that they were told not to eat it? Must have been pretty potent stuff!'

'I think it was from the tree of "good and evil", Son, but – no, wait. It was the tree of "the *knowledge* of good and evil", that was it.'

'Hear that?' spluttered Zak, spinning round to the others. 'It was a tree of *knowledge* – just like the cubes! I'll bet the forbidden cube contains that same knowledge!'

Yes, it made sense. Even Tom was beginning to nod his head like an old sage. He was stubborn all right, but he wasn't stupid, and the more he thought about it the more it seemed to tie in with so much of what they had seen and heard. Yes, the Eden theory was a possible explanation. Unlikely, yes, but very, very possible!

'But if this is true,' said Becky, suddenly alarmed, 'then the people here are in terrible danger!'

Malone laughed. 'I don't suppose a few weeds will hurt them.'

'You don't understand!' she cried. 'I remember something else about the story now. There was no death until Adam and Eve ate the fruit! Don't you see? If Quintay and the others touch that cube they'll all die!'

Captain Malone curled a comforting arm round her shoulders. 'Now steady on, girl . . .'

But her father was looking troubled. 'You know, she's right. That *is* how it ended up.'

'And that's what Micha said!' gasped Zak. 'Remember when he challenged Sath at the meeting this morning? He said something about The Maker telling them not to touch the cube, or – or the day they touched it they'd die!'

'So *that's* why we're here!' muttered Tom – and every face turned towards him, intrigued. 'Well, it's obvious, isn't it! We came to warn them not to make the same mistake as our world did.'

'That's what Micha meant about the book!' shouted Zak.

'What book?' queried his sister.

'Didn't I tell you? Before the meeting, Micha was telling me something about a book that he said held the key to all mysteries – what did he call it? "The Book of The Lamb", that was it! Well, I asked him if he had a copy because I remembered Quintay had given us that riddle about a lamb.

115

But Micha said no, *he* didn't have a copy – but that *we* had! And *then* he said: *"That's why you're here!"'* Zak leapt in the air with a triumphant whoop! 'That's it – he *must* have been talking about the Bible!'

'And that's why *Dad* was brought here,' added Becky, her eyes wide. 'To show Quintay the Bible and to explain to the People's Counsel why they mustn't touch that cube!'

'Now just hang on a minute,' the Colonel cut in. 'Let's get our facts right before this thing gets out of hand. I was sent by Starforce to investigate distress signals in Quasar-Noma, which is half-way across the universe. I don't see any connection between those signals and this planet.'

'But it was the distress calls that led you into the space-warp, Dad. And the same thing happened to us.'

'She's got a point,' said Zak. 'Suppose those signals were set up simply to draw our attention and bring us to Terran?'

The astronaut thought about it for a moment, then shook his head. 'It's too fantastic, Zak.'

But Malone said, 'I think he's got something, Roy. After all, we never found the source of those signals and you've got to admit it is kinda strange that the space-warp spat you out right into Terran's orbit. I mean, the theory does hold up.'

The Colonel nodded. 'OK. But that doesn't explain the SOS. Where did *that* come from?'

The youngsters laughed – that was the easiest part!

'The Maker!' they chorused.

'Or to put it another way,' added Malone, 'God.'

'It all fits!' Becky told him, looping her arm through his. 'Do you see it, Dad?'

Her father eyed her seriously. 'Oh, I see it, honey. I can believe in God easy enough, and I can even accept that he might use foolish men to further his plans – your Grandma did a good job there! – but it's the other side of the coin that's a little disturbing.'

'What do you mean, sir?' asked Tom.

'Well, if God – or, The Maker – brought me here, and the

reason was to warn these people from repeating Adam's mistake, that implies that what made me crash and then lifted the ship into that pit was something very different.' He glanced at them. 'You get my drift?'

Becky was already ahead of him.

'The serpent!' And as she spoke the words she shivered. She moved closer to her father and gazed around into the darkness of the canyon beyond the splash of the flashlight beams. So that's why Eve had felt so spooked! An evil being had been here in this dark and desolate place ... and the sense of its presence had lingered.

She shuddered again. 'Let's get out of here – *now*!'

'Don't worry, we're going,' said Zak, turning away. 'We have to get back to the space-cruiser to pick up the tapes of the Bible in our own library. We must get them to Quintay as soon as possible.'

'If that awful man with the electric shocks hasn't got to them first,' trembled Becky.

'Or Sath,' blurted Tom.

Becky turned to him in alarm. 'Why do you say that?'

'Well, it's obvious,' said the boy. 'The enemy has already convinced *him* about the cube, the way he was ranting and raving at the meeting. I reckon the serpent's signed him up!'

'Don't talk like that,' said the girl. 'Eve's been with him all afternoon. I couldn't bear to think of anything happening to her!'

'Jupiter!' gasped Zak, glancing round. 'Eve was going to show Sath over the cruiser! Oh *no*! Come on, hurry! We don't have a minute to lose!'

The spherical ship leapt into the black sky, lights flashing and programmed at top speed on automatic pilot. Destination: spaceport.

It was a curious sensation, gliding along in the darkness, unable to see where they were going, and they were heartened to recall Micha's assurance that the system included an anti-crash mechanism.

To Colonel Anderson, who as yet knew nothing of Terran's astounding technology, the whole idea was rather unnerving. How ever could you control a spacecraft with thought-waves!

But he had little time to think of such things. This theory about their presence on Terran was absorbing and humbling, not to mention a little frightening. The enemy had already displayed enormous supernatural powers in bringing down *Excalibur* and then incarcerating it in that wretched hole. And then there had been the destruction of the tapes. Colonel Anderson did not relish another encounter with that creature and its fierce anger. The thought threw up some alarming questions.

Just how powerful was the enemy? Did it know that the Colonel was now free and on his way to warn Quintay? Would it seek to intercept him yet again on his curious mission? Had it already sought to destroy the micro-tapes of the Bible stored in the space-cruiser?

And what about The Maker – the God whom his mother had taught him to trust and fear, the Creator of the universe to whom he had prayed as a child – would he intervene?

As the strange Terran ship bore them through the darkness he was aware that over the years he had grown away from the

God of his childhood. In those early years he had known beyond doubt that the great God of heaven and earth was the all-powerful one, the Almighty and Everlasting Father who had set the planets in their orbits and called every star by name. Was he still the same today? If so, why had he allowed the enemy to thwart his divine plan to save these innocent people from the same fate as earth's human race all those years ago in the garden of Eden?

But that, he decided, was rather premature. As Jack Malone was fond of saying: never bury your hopes till you know they're dead.

There was hope for Terran yet. Yes, the enemy had played a devastating hand, knocking his ship out of the sky and even sabotaging Terran's tracking systems so that they failed to notice his arrival on the planet. But God – The Maker – had barely blinked before setting in motion his back-up plan. The evidence of that was all around him in the shape of his family and friends. It was all quite remarkable, and very wonderful.

But those thoughts could wait. The battle wasn't over yet, and the words of his military training came back to him with force: never underestimate your enemy.

Presently they saw the lights of the city on the distant horizon and at last had something to set their sights on.

'Not long now,' said Zak. 'Then we can check out those tapes.'

'I *do* hope they're still there,' murmured Becky, cuddled against her father and feeling rather sleepy after the day's activity. She hoped the Colonel wouldn't object to her yawning on duty.

They were all feeling tired as the ship zoomed the last few miles to the spaceport. But they soon stirred at the sight that lay before them. The city, staggering in its beauty by daylight, was equally stunning by night. Lit up in the most dazzling and brilliant colours, the whole city complex glowed and shone.

'Like something out of the most extravagant dream,' was

how Colonel Anderson summed up his first glimpse of the metropolis. There was trouble ahead in this beautiful place, they realized that; and maybe tomorrow the dream would become a nightmare. But they were glad to be back.

'Look, there's another ship taking off,' said Tom, and Zak wondered about contacting the spaceport authorities for landing permission. That was unnecessary, however – the ship was beginning to make its own adjustments for the final approach.

His father leaned forward, curious. 'Don't you have to check in with Control, son?'

Zak grinned. 'I think the automatic pilot just did! We were coming in on one air-lane and now we've been directed to another – see?'

The Colonel nodded. 'So the spaceport's activities are co-ordinated by a central computer.'

'Something like that. But going by what we've learned of their technology so far, the whole system would be far more sophisticated than anything we've ever dreamed up on earth.'

'These boys are light years ahead, Roy,' added Malone. 'You won't *believe* some of their tricks!'

'I'm not sure that I believe *any* of it,' said the astronaut. 'I keep thinking that maybe soon I'll wake up back home in Texas!'

'Want me to pinch you, Dad?' offered Becky.

Her father smiled down at her, but said nothing.

'There's the cruiser, Colonel,' announced Tom. 'Bet you never thought you'd see *that* again, sir!'

The astronaut gazed down on his ship – his own personal spacecraft. Tom was right – he *had* doubted that he would ever see this machine again. *Or* his children and friends. And he was filled with thankfulness. When this business was over he would put his own affairs straight with The Maker. It was about time, he told himself.

'She's looking good, son,' he said.

'Performs pretty well, too,' boasted Tom. 'We all reckon

she could outrun even *Excalibur*.'

The Colonel laughed. 'Well, we'll have to see about that! If we can get *Excalibur* patched up I might just race you home!'

Captain Malone said, 'Oh you'll get her patched up all right. These guys will probably rebuild it from scratch in twenty minutes!' And he told his buddy about the amazing silver spheres which had come to their aid when the cruiser's engines had died on them.

Shaking his head in wonder, the astronaut turned to his daughter. 'Maybe you *had* better pinch me, honey!'

They put down on the apron close to the cruiser and Zak said, 'Right, let's check those tapes!'

Tom was first out, with Zak and Becky on his tail, all of them dashing for the hatchway. Up the steps they went, the outer door instantly sliding open, and one after the other they fell inside. The lights blinked on, and then they were through the air-lock door and chasing through the ship and into the relaxation bay, their hearts pounding and throats dry.

Were the tapes safe?

'Please, *please* let them be there!' breathed Becky as Tom fumbled excitedly with the video-library controls.

'Come on!' grumbled Zak and pushed the younger boy aside, his fingers moving quickly to the controls, programming the machine to locate the vital evidence.

By the time Malone and Colonel Anderson strode into the bay seconds later they had the answer.

Their faces would have been enough to tell the tale, but Becky cried out, 'They've gone! The tapes have gone!'

'Are you sure?' roared Malone. 'Here, let me check.'

But there was no mistake. The micro-tapes of the Bible had been removed.

'Oh no!' wailed Zak. 'What do we do now?'

Colonel Anderson shook his head. 'He did it again. That monster did it again!'

'It must have been Sath!' said Tom. 'He's been in here with Eve and taken the tapes while she wasn't looking. The serpent must have put him up to it! I'll bet that . . .'

'Listen!' Zak cut in and motioned them to be quiet. 'Did you hear that noise?' he murmured. 'I'm sure someone's coming!'

Yes, there was the sound of movement down by the hatchway! There was an intruder aboard!

Colonel Anderson whipped the hand-laser from his belt and went quietly to the doorway, peering outside. Slowly he raised the weapon . . . 'OK, come out with your hands above your head – nice and easy . . .'

The others glanced nervously at each other. Was a laser really any use against the man with the electric powers? Had he hunted them down to finish them off? He had already grabbed both sets of tapes. The only thing now standing between the success and failure of his fiendish plan was the people in that room. It stood to reason that he would try to destroy them. In that desperate moment they realized they should have been more careful – a guard should have been posted outside to warn them. But it was too late now.

'Don't shoot,' called a voice. 'It's me – Micha.'

Becky almost collapsed with relief and Zak blurted out, 'Oh, thank goodness!'

'It's OK, Roy,' Malone confirmed. 'This one's on *our* side!'

Colonel Anderson lowered the hand-laser but kept it primed, just in case. He was quite sure that their enemy was capable of deceiving them by imitating the voice of a friend.

But it was all right. Smiling somewhat apprehensively, Micha stepped out with his hands held wide.

'Oh, Micha!' breathed Becky. 'You sure gave us a nasty turn! Why did you come creeping into the ship like that?'

'I'm sorry,' smiled the pilot. 'I didn't mean to alarm you. I take it you have *reason* to be alarmed?' He turned to face her father, reaching out a friendly hand. 'You must be Colonel Anderson. Sorry we had to meet under such circumstances.'

'My fault,' said the astronaut, shaking hands. 'I'm a little jumpy after my ordeal. I think we'd better tell you about it.'

122

It was a muddly explanation with each one of them chipping in parts of the story. Micha appeared quite horrified at what they had to tell, and he sympathized greatly with their fears. Clearly they were distressed over the loss of the tapes – or rather, the *apparent* loss of them!

While Zak was still telling how they'd discovered the vital tapes missing, Micha reached into his tunic . . . and when he withdrew his hand, there they were!

'The tapes?' gasped Becky. 'Of the Bible?'

Their friend nodded, a huge smile on his face.

'But – *how*?' gurgled Tom.

'Simple. I got here before Sath and removed them myself.'

'But how did you *know* about the tapes?' asked Malone. 'None of *us* knew till we found Roy.'

The pilot laughed. 'There's no mystery about it. Like you, I heard the inner voice.'

'You mean The Maker *told* you to come and get them?' Becky was finding it hard to believe what she was hearing.

Micha nodded. 'Is that so surprising?'

'Then you knew about Sath, too,' said Tom.

'And that's why you couldn't come with us to the canyon,' added Zak.

'That – and to keep an eye on Eve,' said Micha.

'Is she all right?' blurted the boy.

'Of course. I told you she would be. She's at Quintay's. I took her there after Sath abandoned her.'

'What!' roared Zak. 'What d'you mean, abandoned her?'

'Exactly that. Once he'd discovered that the tapes were missing he became extremely angry and just stormed out. Left her here on her own – except that I was hiding through there on the flight deck. I heard it all; she was really quite upset.'

Zak almost exploded. 'Why, the dirty, rotten . . . He just used her, that's all!'

'I'm afraid so,' said Micha. 'But she's fine now. We sat down and had a good, long talk. I explained a few things to her and she seemed a lot better. She said she owed you an apology, Zak.'

The boy looked awkward. 'Aw, that doesn't matter. So long as she's all right.'

The pilot nodded, smiling.

Colonel Anderson studied the friendly face for a moment.

'There's just one thing I don't understand, Micha. How did you get in here for those tapes? The outer door opens only when one of *us* approaches.' He indicated a stud on the collar of his flying-suit. 'This gives off an electronic signal.'

The pilot shrugged. 'I didn't think about how I would get in, Colonel. I assumed that if The Maker wanted me to remove the tapes for safe-keeping he would take care of a little thing like that. The door simply slid open when I approached, and slid shut when I left. But does all that matter?' He held up the micro-tapes, smiling. 'Surely these are what count: The Book of The Lamb.'

An excited smile flashed between Zak and Becky. They *had* been right: the two books were one and the same! But who or what was the lamb? And what about the riddle Quintay had given them?

'I think those questions can wait,' Micha told them. 'You'll have your answers soon enough. Now shouldn't we be going?'

'I guess so,' said Zak, 'but I'd rather like to run the tapes through the machine first.' He turned to his father. 'To read the Eden story for myself.'

The others agreed.

'That's not a bad idea,' nodded the Colonel. 'A refresher might be just the thing if we've got to explain all this to your friend Quintay.'

Micha said he had transport outside and would wait for them there. Tom thought that was a good idea because the pilot could keep a look-out for trouble at the same time.

'The last thing we want is that character with the red eyeballs barging in here,' he said.

124

Minutes later they were gathered round the relaxation bay's communal screen – normally reserved for movies and computer games – reading through the first chapters of the Bible. It was a story to which, hours earlier, they wouldn't have given a second thought: the story of how the universe had come into being ... of how planet earth and everything on it had begun ... and of how a single, rebellious act of the first man and woman had destroyed the purity of that creation. In short – an account of The Maker's triumph ... and mankind's downfall.

Only hours ago it had been a fable, a fairy story, a myth, a half-forgotten tale. But now, how different! Now the story was all too real. Now it was happening all over again on another world in another galaxy. The lovely garden, the forbidden knowledge, the words of the enemy – on Terran they were seeing the scenes unfold all over again.

The only difference between the two situations, it seemed, was that on Terran the enemy had waited much longer before slithering into the garden with his deceptions and lies. Was it possible that he had purposely been kept in check by The Maker until earth-people had grown up sufficiently to find their own way to Terran through the space-warp? It was certainly true that a manned spacecraft from earth had never before travelled as far as Quasar-Noma ... and that The Maker appeared to work and care for his people in remarkable ways.

Whatever the truth, they were caught up in the middle of it and the Creator of the universe had put them there.

That was remarkable enough. But what really shook them was that it seemed almost as though the ending of *this* Eden story had been left to them. *They* had been entrusted to bring knowledge not to be found in any of those amazing cubes to Terran. This vital knowledge alone could expose the subtle tactics of the enemy and alert the faltering members of the People's Counsel to the fate which awaited them if they chose to ignore The Maker's commands.

It was an enormous responsibility! But they would not fail. They were determined. They would rush the tapes to Quintay – and surely with that weapon in his hands he would at last be able to persuade his colleagues of their folly and rescue Terran from the brink of disaster.

There was no time to be lost! They must get the micro-tapes to Quintay as soon as possible!

'But how will he understand them?' questioned the Colonel as Zak quickly rewound the tapes. 'Will we have to read them to him?'

'I doubt it, Dad. I'm sure their technology can cope with a simple translation problem.'

'If not,' said Becky, 'I guess The Maker will find a way. Oh, do hurry, Zak!'

Micha drove them into the city at top speed, haring through the streets and round the bends in a spectacular display of night-driving which Tom declared 'positively egg-citing'!

If Colonel Anderson was a little apprehensive, that was only to be expected of a novice. The more experienced egg-traveller could afford to relax – although none of them was brave enough not to wince when they shot through that solid wall again! The Colonel was suitably bewildered, thanks to the conspiracy of silence which had kept secret the fact that their brakes wouldn't actually be applied until they were inside Shara's lounge!

Fortunately there was no one standing in the way and they piled out to a warm reception. There were broad smiles all round, and a special welcome from Quintay and Shara for Zak and Becky's father.

'We're so thankful you're safe, Colonel,' beamed Quintay.

'Thank you,' said the astronaut. 'I *was* beginning to wonder whether I would ever see a friendly face again!'

'Yes,' blurted Tom, 'he was held prisoner by an evil thing with red eyes and thunderbolts up its sleeve!'

'We think it was the enemy!' babbled Becky. 'He destroyed Dad's Bible and we think he's tricked Sath into working for him.'

'What was that about Sath?' said a girl's voice from the doorway. '*I* can tell you a thing or two about him!'

'Eve!' chorused the youngsters, and they rushed to greet her.

'Eve, you were right about there being an enemy,' Becky told her.

'We're sorry we didn't believe you,' added Tom.

'And *I'm* sorry about this afternoon,' said Zak, putting an arm round her shoulders.

She smiled at him. 'Don't be, Zak. You were right and I was – I was a fool.'

He shook his head. 'It wasn't your fault – you were just deceived.'

She nodded. 'It's strange, though, isn't it – considering I was the only one who thought there *was* an enemy.'

Colonel Anderson said, 'Not really – not in view of your name, young lady.' He stretched out a hand. 'Nice to meet you, Eve.'

She shook hands, smiling coyly. 'Oh, er, Colonel Anderson . . .' And then she looked at him, puzzled. 'What did you mean, sir – about my name?'

'Yes,' said Quintay, 'this all sounds very intriguing. What is the significance of Eve's name? And did somebody mention an enemy? Exactly what *is* going on?'

The astronaut turned to the old man and noticed for the first time how brightly his eyes shone.

'It's rather a long story, sir. We have some tapes we think you should play – tapes of a very old and sacred book. But maybe first we should tell you *our* part of the story.' He turned to Zak. 'Do you want to begin, son?'

Quintay and Shara listened with amazement. To think that what was happening on Terran was almost a re-run of events on earth all those thousands of years ago!

And to learn about the enemy! Why, from the dawn of their history they had not so much as *imagined* the existence of such a creature! This would certainly explain the attitude of Sath and the others; no wonder they were rebelling if they were listening to him.

But surely not for much longer? Surely they would give up such foolishness once they had heard for themselves what their guests had to say and studied the tragic lessons of that other garden?

How thankful Quintay and Shara were that The Maker had not allowed this enemy to go undetected; how grateful they were for the timely arrival of their friends from earth. There was so much they had not understood, especially the awful consequences of disobeying The Maker's command. 'You shall die!' was the warning, but death was an unknown quantity to them.

Now they understood the meaning of the terrible curse, striking decay and destruction not only into their own bodies – that was bad enough – but also into every area of their perfect world. All forms of life would suffer: people, the animal kingdom, the plant world . . . at every level perfection would give way to corruption. Creation itself would topple and fall, just as it had on planet earth.

But as if this was not reason enough never to touch that forbidden cube, Quintay then learned from the micro-tapes of what seemed to him an even greater curse.

He turned from the small screen on which he was studying the Genesis story, a great sadness in his eyes. His voice was hoarse with emotion.

'It's unthinkable! Unbearable!' He turned to his wife. 'My dear, they were put out of the garden!'

Shara's hand flew to her mouth, masking her horror, but her eyes said it all.

'Can you imagine it?' muttered the old man. 'To be driven from the garden by The Maker himself.'

Tears clouded Shara's eyes. 'You mean, never to hear his voice again? Never to talk with him?'

'It certainly sounds like it,' came the unhappy reply. He turned to Colonel Anderson. 'Is that so? Was the relationship between your people and The Maker broken beyond repair?'

The astronaut hesitated. 'I, er – I really don't know. Some people on our planet worship God . . .'

'Only *some* of your people?'

The Colonel looked awkward and glanced at Jack Malone for support – but it was Becky who spoke.

'Quintay, there's no point in us hiding anything from you, or trying to pretend that things are better than they are. Our world is – well, very different from yours. Here you have a small community – a family – and you all live at peace with one another because you all have a wonderful friendship with The Maker. On earth it isn't like that. We have many millions of people – billions, in fact – and the truth is that very few know anything at all about The Maker.'

'We don't know much about living in peace, either,' said Eve. She glanced at Quintay with a faint, rueful smile. 'I'm afraid we've made rather a mess of things.'

'What do you mean?' asked the old man.

She glanced at Colonel Anderson, not wanting to speak out of turn. He nodded, and she continued.

'When we left our planet, sir, there was a terrible war going on, and for all we know it may be raging still.'

'Unless they've all blown each other up!' offered Tom, but

that drew scathing looks which silenced him.

Quintay turned to Eve. 'You'll have to forgive my ignorance, but what is war?'

They could have wept! Quintay wasn't ignorant; he was innocent. There was a great difference. What must it be like to live in a world where war was unheard of; a world which had never known violence because it knew none of the things that led to it! Anger, pride, greed, jealousy, fear, selfishness ... none of these was known on Terran, and not likely to be, as long as the relationship with The Maker remained unchanged.

What a contrast to their own world – a contrast depending on a single act of disobedience so long ago.

If only they could put the clock back and change earth's history! Such a thing was not possible, of course. But they could at least help to make sure that earth's tragedy did not become Terran's. It was painful and embarrassing to admit the awful things about their own world, but they would gladly do so to save Quintay and his family from the same fate.

'War?' said Eve, in answer to Quintay's question. 'It's when one group of people turn against another and start killing them because they can't get what they want by any other means.'

Quintay and Shara stared at them in horrified disbelief.

'I'm afraid it was happening on a very large scale when we left home,' said Captain Malone. 'You see, our countries have built very powerful weapons – explosives that can kill millions of people at once.' He glanced down. 'My own family was killed in such a war.'

Compassion filled Quintay's eyes. 'My dear Captain ... I'm so sorry. This is terrible, all of it. Simply terrible.'

Colonel Anderson said, 'It's ironic, but even our being here started with the quest for military advantage. I don't know if Zak told you, but my mission was to track down the source of distress signals that we were monitoring from deep space. If we'd found that those signals were emanating from another world with military capability our leaders would have made every effort to win the friendship and support of those people, because if *we* didn't do that our enemy would. We just couldn't afford to let that happen. We believe the balance of power on earth would depend on it.'

Quintay shook his head, quite unable to understand all this.

'This is a result of Adam's fall?' he asked.

'That's the theory,' said the Colonel, and then he remembered something – a whisper from his childhood, a fleeting memory of those Bible stories. 'In fact you can trace the act of murder right to Adam and Eve's door. They had two sons, Cain and Abel. One of them killed the other because he was jealous of him. I forget which was which, but you'll find it right there in the tapes; just read on a little further.'

The old man nodded sombrely. 'I should very much like to read on, Colonel. In fact, I think I must. There may be other things I should know. Is that so?' His eyes fell on Captain Malone, who shifted awkwardly in his seat.

'No good looking at me, sir. I'm afraid I've not so much as turned the cover of a Bible. Few of us have.'

Quintay eyed him seriously. 'Then who knows,' he said, 'perhaps I shall learn something to *your* advantage, too.'

They had a meal together and then Quintay retired to his room to study the tapes while the others settled back for a relaxing evening. Daffon and Briod engaged the boys in a complex-looking strategy game – 'three-dimensional chess' Tom called it – and Becky became engrossed in Shara's brightly-coloured tapestries. The Colonel and Malone spent the evening deep in conversation with Micha.

Eventually, however, they could stifle the yawns no longer, and they all decided to turn in. Micha left, and very soon the house was in darkness, except for a soft light in Quintay's room.

If they had listened they would have heard the old man muttering to himself now and then. 'Well, well! I'd never imagined!' ... 'Oh, how tragic!' ... 'Isn't that wonderful?' ... 'Just wait till they hear about this!'

Quintay did not go to bed that night. The Bible, he discovered, was a long and absorbing book. It was quite unlike anything he had ever read, but then he had never read anything directly inspired by The Maker before.

But more than that, he discovered another side to his Creator. It was a story that astonished, saddened and thrilled him by turn.

And The Maker, he learned, had a son.

'Did *you* know?' he asked his guests the next morning – and they had never seen his eyes shine so brightly.

At first only blank stares met his question, but then those long-ago Bible stories came to the Colonel's rescue once again.

'You mean Jesus?'

The bright eyes glowed. 'You *do* know!'

'Oh, we've all heard of Jesus,' said Becky, grinning. 'Every kid learns about the world's great teachers in college.'

'But we never heard him called the son of God,' said Zak, and then he glanced at his sister. 'Or did we?'

His father smiled. 'That'll be Grandma's influence again. In college they teach Christ only as the world's most famous philosopher.'

'You *do* know about him, Colonel,' said Quintay. 'You even know that he was called the Christ, God's chosen one!'

'Well, I wouldn't say I know that much, Quintay.' He laughed. 'It's a long time since I sat on Momma's knee!'

'What was that you said about the chosen one, Quintay?' asked Tom. 'What does that mean?'

The old fellow's face was radiant. This was the moment he'd been waiting for.

'My dear Tom, Colonel – all of you. I have the most wonderful news for you.' And he paused, waiting until he had their full attention. 'Yesterday I was deeply disturbed to hear how the relationship between Adam and The Maker was broken and how he was driven from the garden. My friends, my heart was crushed, for I don't know how I would survive if *my* friendship with The Maker were suddenly cut off. I'm not even sure I would want to. To me that would be a most miserable existence; as I've said before, I should prefer the sun to stop shining.

'That left me with a very big question, particularly when I heard about the terrible things – wars and suchlike – which have resulted from Adam's folly. You see, I know how loving and gracious The Maker is, and I couldn't escape this question: why didn't he do something about it? I couldn't begin to imagine that he would have washed his hands of your whole human race; that doesn't sound like him at all. Surely, I thought, because he is wise and compassionate he could find a way out – an escape route from Adam's curse; some means of restoring the bond of peace and unity between himself and his creation?' He paused, glancing at each of them in turn while a tender smile crept over his face. 'And then, as I read that most wonderful book last night, I discovered that that is just what he did. He sent a second Adam – your Bible calls him the *last* Adam; another perfect man, only this time that man was also God himself.'

'Jesus?' asked Eve. It was a question that was on all their lips.

The old man nodded. 'Jesus – The Maker's own son. *He* has made it possible for you and all your people to be reconciled to The Maker – restored to the relationship which Adam and Eve enjoyed with him before they disobeyed him . . . indeed, the relationship which our people here on Terran still enjoy to this very day.'

Becky said, 'But how, Quintay? What did Jesus do to put things right?'

'He gave his life,' came the simple reply.

They all stared, and the Colonel said, 'You mean, when he

was crucified?'

'It was his father's plan,' Quintay told him. 'The Maker accepted his death as settlement of Adam's debt. Do you see it? Because Jesus died you may all now live.'

Zak looked puzzled. 'Gee, that seems pretty hard on Jesus.'

'He gave his life of his own free will,' said the old fellow. 'Besides, there was no other way. It's clearly explained in your Bible. The penalty for sin – for disobeying God – is death. His life for yours. In the old days a lamb was offered in sacrifice . . .'

'Hey, did you hear that!' gasped Zak, glancing at the others. 'Remember the riddle? About the lamb?'

'And the *Book* of the Lamb, too!' said Tom. 'Micha *said* it was the same as the Bible!' He turned to Quintay. 'You mean that *Jesus* is the Lamb?'

'I do indeed. It's all there in the book. You'll find that one of the names given to The Maker's son – and there are many – is "the Lamb of God".' He glanced at his notes. 'Listen to this: "God paid a ransom to save you from the impossible road to heaven which your fathers tried to take" – that would refer to the old, inadequate animal sacrifices, of course – "and the ransom he paid was not mere gold or silver . . . but he paid for you with the precious lifeblood of Christ, the sinless, spotless Lamb of God."'

Becky said, 'That *does* make sense of the riddle at last. We couldn't even begin to understand what The Maker was getting at.'

'How does the riddle go?' asked her father, but she had forgotten the words and had to look to Zak.

'Er, let me think – "only he may enter . . . who . . . who knows by name the Lamb." That's it.'

Becky turned to her father. 'You see, we wanted to go into the garden when The Maker was there . . .'

'But we couldn't,' said Eve. 'At least, not unless we understood the riddle.'

Quintay said, 'I see it myself, now. It simply means that if you people from earth wish to enter The Maker's presence you need to come by way of the Lamb.' He glanced around at them. 'The book makes it very clear: there is no other way for the relationship to be restored.'

Captain Malone said slowly, 'It's tragic that the son should have to die; it must have broken The Maker's heart.'

'It did,' came the flat reply. 'But that wasn't the end of the story, I'm glad to say.'

'Christ rose from the dead ...' said the Colonel, remembering.

'And ascended into heaven,' Quintay finished for him. Then a twinkle appeared in his eye. 'And I'll tell you something else you didn't know: he's going to return to your planet some day – to set up his kingdom. As it were, to plant a new garden!'

'Is he really?' asked Eve, smiling.

'I'm *so* glad you told us, Quintay,' said Becky.

Malone shook his head in wonder. 'Say, I never knew any of this stuff. Why, that book is – fantastic!'

'Fantastic, and true!' beamed the old fellow. 'You can take my word for that ... because I'm on very good terms with the author!'

They all laughed, and Quintay turned to Becky and Eve first, and then the others. 'Let's have breakfast,' he said.

15

Later that morning, shortly before the meeting was due to begin, they left the house and walked up through the beautiful garden, happy and relaxed. It was a glorious day, the bright sun painting the blooms and blossom in their brightest colours, and just the merest hint of a breeze to carry the fragrance of the scented bushes across their path.

It really was the most delightful place, thought the visitors, and Becky particularly appreciated it now that she was able to stroll between the trees arm-in-arm with her father. 'Unbelievable!' was the Colonel's remark. 'I thought Paradise existed only in dreams and storybooks.'

But no one that morning could have been quite so appreciative of the garden as Quintay. Today he valued it more highly than ever before . . . because never before had he contemplated losing it. But he did not dwell on this unhappy thought, for thanks to The Maker's intervention in sending help from earth he was confident that this miserable fate could now be avoided. Let Sath and the others bring out all their arguments for holding that forbidden cube – Quintay was sure they would abandon their misguided quest once they'd heard the Eden story for themselves.

Yes, he felt ready for anything! Anything, perhaps, except the inner voice that spoke so clearly to him as they covered the last few metres to the round building where all the other Counsel members were in their seats, waiting for the proceedings to begin. That voice truly took him by surprise.

He turned to Colonel Anderson, slightly perplexed.

'Colonel, I don't wish to appear impolite, but could I ask you not to come into the building with us just now. I know this is rather sudden, but I've just had it impressed upon me to ask you to wait out here until I call you. Would that be all right? I know it must be a bit of a surprise.'

The astronaut smiled. He had taken a tip from Jack Malone and was quickly learning to accept surprises as routine on this planet.

'Sure. I'll just sit out here and enjoy the sun till you need me. Just call and I'll come running.'

Becky volunteered to keep her father company, and so did Eve. She was in no hurry to set eyes on Sath again! But the astronaut wouldn't hear of it.

Moments later they were taking their seats, the glowing tower of cubes was descending into the floor, and the murmur of conversation faded into a hush.

Quintay glanced around the circle of faces with a satisfied smile. The meeting had begun. He rose quickly to his feet.

'Gentlemen, I have some very good news for you. I believe that as from today our differences concerning the forbidden cube will be resolved.'

'At last!' called one of the members.

'But to whose advantage?' queried another.

'To everybody's,' said the old man emphatically. 'As will be made very clear to you once you have all heard what our friends here have to say. Yesterday, as you know, they had no idea why they had been brought to Terran; indeed, all any of us knew was that The Maker had requested their presence at this meeting.' He paused. 'But that was yesterday, my friends, and a great deal has happened in the intervening hours. Shortly our visitors will tell you for themselves how they discovered the purpose behind their journey to our world, but allow me to outline for you the startling discoveries that I myself have made since these people came among us.'

There was a murmur of surprise. Then he continued, 'Firstly, I have learned that long ago on planet earth there was a garden not unlike our own, and two people not unlike ourselves. Their names were Adam and Eve. They were placed in the garden by The Maker – or, as the earth people call him, God. Now these people lived off the fruit from the trees in the garden, but there was one tree whose fruit they were not allowed to touch. The Maker told them that if they disobeyed they would die. However, there came into the garden a creature whose will was opposed to The Maker – a creature called the serpent. Now this serpent . . .'

'One moment, Quintay,' interrupted Sath. 'I hesitate to question the integrity of our visitors, but are we to assume that your case is to rest upon this – this parody of our own dignified world? And mere hearsay at that! I really must challenge the authenticity of such an unlikely . . .'

'Enough of that,' snapped Quintay. 'This is neither parody nor hearsay, but well-documented fact. The account is recorded here' – he held up the micro-tapes – 'in earth's most sacred book, the Bible.'

'Is that your "evidence"?' scoffed Sath.

'Allow Quintay to finish,' called Micha. 'Hear him out.'

'Why? To fill our ears with fables? How do we know we can trust this book? Why should we pay any heed to what may well be a string of fanciful fiction?'

'You paid it enough heed yesterday!' stormed Eve, leaping to her feet, and every eye turned towards her. 'You wouldn't stop pestering me to show you the Bible in our library aboard the space-cruiser!'

Sath flushed slightly. 'A mere passing interest in your culture, my dear. You don't for one minute think that I was *seriously* interested in reviewing such fantasy.'

Zak could take no more; he already had a score to settle with this man. Jumping to his feet he cried out, 'Well, *somebody* on this planet is interested in the Bible, I can tell you that!' He glanced quickly round the circle. 'Listen to me, all of you. We *do* know why we've been brought to your planet. At the beginning of our own history on earth our people went through exactly the same crisis you're facing right now and our forefathers made the wrong decision. They *ate* the forbidden fruit, just like some of you here want to hold that cube, but we're here to warn you against it. When Adam and Eve rebelled against God ...'

'I object!' roared Sath.

'Shut up!' snapped Zak. 'I haven't finished. Now please listen, everyone ...'

'How *dare* you speak to me like that!' boomed Sath, and his face darkened to a terrible red.

But Zak was getting fired up, too. 'And who do you think *you* are! I'll *tell* you who you are – you're a traitor who's listened to the serpent. You're working for the enemy!'

'Order, order!' cried Quintay, but Sath was leaping up and down with rage and there was no holding him now.

'I'll warn you just once more, boy – be careful what you say to me!'

'Sit down, both of you!' shouted Quintay.

'What's going on in here?' yelled a new voice, and every eye turned towards the door. Colonel Anderson stood there glaring at his son. 'Zak, is that you raising your voice in ...' The words fell from his lips like stone as the astronaut suddenly caught sight of Sath.

Quintay stared. 'What is it, Colonel?'

A trembling finger pointed at Sath.

'Him!' He glanced at Quintay. 'He's the one who destroyed the tapes! He's the enemy!'

Becky screamed, 'Look at his eyes!'

The eyes were blazing red – fiery red – and an enormous growl now escaped from Sath's lips. He swung round at the Colonel, pointing at him across the room.

'*You* are *dead*!'

Immediately a bolt of fire leapt from the end of his finger – but with a speed that amazed everyone Micha flew from his seat and intercepted the missile. He caught the full force of the bolt in his chest and was thrown back against the Colonel.

'Micha!' cried Eve.

But instantly he was back on his feet and thrusting an accusing finger towards the enemy. Incredibly, he was unharmed.

'Deceiver, your time is up!' he shouted. 'Father of lies, you are found out! Satan, you are exposed!'

An evil roar suddenly filled that room and before their eyes the most horrifying metamorphosis took place. Exploding from his human disguise, the enemy quickly grew into the terrifying, evil monster that he was, howling with an anger that shook the very foundations.

Beneath him the people scattered, failing even to notice that Micha too was changing – growing in height and girth to equal his enemy, and shining with a dazzling light that challenged the darkness pouring from Satan's mouth.

'So it is you – *Michael*!' hissed the monster. 'He has sent you against me.'

But as he spoke, a huge, flaming sword appeared in Michael's hand. 'The Maker orders you to be gone!' he cried.

'Then I defy him!' roared the beast.

With an almighty crash the roof split open as the two giant figures grew taller still... The walls shattered and fell. The building splintered like matchwood.

With screams and shouts of alarm, the people scrambled out through the rubble and raced panic-stricken for the cover of the trees. Miraculously, no one had been hurt.

When they turned to look again they could scarcely believe their eyes. The two frightening figures now towered over them, poised for battle.

'You are already defeated!' cried Michael as he wielded the mighty sword. But the adversary roared again and raised his huge, gnarled fists.

'The sky!' cried Quintay. 'What is happening to the sky?'

A great darkness was sweeping in over the garden, blocking out the sun and sending an icy, howling wind chasing through the trees. There was a rolling of thunder ... lightning flashed ... lights flared across the sky. The two figures in the eye of the storm were locked in fierce combat.

The sword flashed, the fists crashed down, the blade struck home ... A piercing scream rang out as the terrible monster toppled. But a moment later he was up again, leaping into the black sky to pluck a flash of lightning from the air. He hurled the crackling bolt at the angel, dashing him to the ground and sending the flaming sword spinning into the darkness.

'The powers of darkness are against you!' roared the enemy – and summoning all his evil strength he brought both fists down upon Michael's neck.

An agonized scream rocked the heavens as the warrior fell limp. With victory within his grasp the monster reached into the stars for the flaming sword. His eyes burned with the fires of hell itself as he lifted the blade, poised to plunge it into Michael's heart.

'No!' cried Zak. 'No, Micha, don't die! *Don't die!*'

As the sword flashed down for the fatal blow, Michael the warrior-angel flew from the enemy's grasp and shot up into the heavens, feet together, arms outstretched. Hovering above the monster's head, his body began to glow with a strange and blinding light.

'He – he's making the shape of a cross,' muttered Tom, but in that violent storm his voice was snatched away on the wind.

As the thunder crashed and the flaming lights tore overhead, Satan growled again... But now it seemed he could only shield his eyes and shake an angry fist.

'S-something's happening,' muttered Eve. 'Something's changing.' The storm was dying away. High above them the evil creature could no longer fight ... only resist.

But he would not resist much longer, for as they gazed at the frightening spectacle the bright light of the cross began changing to a deep red.

A cry of torment broke from the evil one as he cowered beneath it. And somewhere there were voices in the sky, chanting a single word: 'Victory!' they called. 'Victory!

141

Victory! Victory!'

'*No*!' screamed the enemy, shrinking away, yet still shaking a defiant fist.

Then 'The blood of the Lamb!' came the cry.

Instantly the creature fell, writhing in agony, screaming in torment.

Then the scream died – and he was gone.

Banished for ever from the garden.

High above the watchers the sky lightened and the sun broke through. They strained their eyes to catch a last glimpse of the glowing cross, of Micha. But there was nothing to be seen.

In the garden there was little sign of the battle that had been fought. As the people came out from among the trees they were amazed to see everything looking quite normal. Everything, that is, except the shattered Counsel chamber. That would have to be rebuilt.

'But no matter,' said Quintay as he and Malone stood inspecting the damage. He shifted an obstructing timber and turned to the Captain with a gentle smile. 'This is all that counts.' And he pointed to the broken circle of desks. 'See – the cubes are still standing!'

A great deal happened in the next few days. Quintay called a gathering of all Terran's people and explained what had taken place in the garden. He also publicly reaffirmed the Counsel's unanimous agreement that the forbidden cube should never, ever be touched!

Then a very grand banquet was held in honour of all their friends from earth.

But from that time onwards the visitors began to think more and more of home. Terran's engineers lifted *Excalibur* from that dark hole and moved it to the spaceport where they repaired all the damage and overhauled the engines, ready for the long journey back to earth.

Meanwhile Quintay gave them all a guided tour of the city

and flew them out over the beautiful countryside to see more of the planet and its creatures.

On the morning of their departure, as they gathered on the spaceport apron, Quintay pressed the tapes of 'The Book of The Lamb' into Zak's hand.

'You'll be needing these,' he said, his bright eyes shining. 'All of you! They're surely the most precious thing your people own.'

The boy nodded – but for once could find no words to reply.

The girls came to him and he reached out his hand. But they threw their arms around him, tears rolling down their cheeks.

'We'll miss you,' Eve said. 'Thank you for everything.'

'And thanks for *this*!' chuckled Tom, who had gone to say goodbye to Daffon and Briod and been presented with their three-dimensional chess set.

Quintay laughed. 'Now that's appropriate.'

'It is?'

'Yes,' said the old man. 'It's your move now.'

The crowd that had gathered to see them off cheered as they turned on the steps of the ships to wave their final farewell.

Minutes later *Excalibur* was hurtling down the runway, zooming up over the shining city and out into the yawning sky. The space-cruiser followed. Together the ships soared up out of the atmosphere, leaving behind them a group of figures who stood watching until the spacecraft were just a memory.

'Come along, my dear,' said Quintay. 'We'd best be getting back. I have a feeling there are a few things I should put on tape myself.' He smiled. 'I think I'll call it "The Book of The Garden" – for the children, you know.'

Shara returned his smile, her eyes full of tears.

On the flight-deck of the cruiser Eve sat gazing up at the screens and watching Terran slide away from them. What a world it had turned out to be, and what a contrast to her own planet earth.

'I wonder if the fighting will have stopped by now?' she murmured.

Aboard *Excalibur* Zak and Becky were flying with their father, the three of them crewing a Starforce ship for the first time – a dream come true. But they had seen so many dreams fulfilled in the past days that this one passed without comment.

At the controls Colonel Anderson leaned forward and entered the co-ordinates for the space-warp into the computers. He turned to Zak.

'Want to take the helm, Son?'

'Who, me? You know I'm not familiar with this model, Dad.'

'Well, there's a first time for everything,' he grinned. 'And I'm sure you can handle it. I heard a whisper that you're now a fully-fledged space-pilot – is that right?'

Zak glanced at him, amused. In all the excitement he had quite forgotten. He reached into his breast-pocket and drew out the official Starforce card that Commander Fairburn had presented to him on the moon. So long ago it seemed now. He grinned and passed the card to his father.

'You're right, Dad – I got my wings.'

'And come to think of it,' said Becky, remembering, 'that's how this whole adventure got started!'